I0791865

Sweet Beginnings

HONEYSUCKLE TEXAS ★ BOOK 1

CHRIS KENISTON

Indie House Publishing

Indie House Publishing

MORE BOOKS
By Chris Keniston

Honeysuckle Texas
Sweet Beginnings
Sweet Surprise
Sweet Temptation
Sweet Deal
Sweet Obsession
Sweet Tomorrows
Sweet Redemption

The Billionaire Barons of Texas
Just One Date
Just One Spark
Just One Dance
Just One Take
Just One Taste
Just One Shot
Just One Chance
Just One Mistake
Just One Family
Just One Rodeo
Just One Surprise
Just One Look

Hart Land
Heather
Lily
Violet
Iris
Hyacinth
Rose
Calytrix
Zinnia

Poppy
Picture Perfect

Farraday Country
Adam
Brooks
Connor
Declan
Ethan
Finn
Grace
Hannah
Ian
Jamison
Keeping Eileen
Loving Chloe
Morgan
Neil
Owen
Paxton
Quinn

Honeymoon Series
Honeymoon for One
Honeymoon for Three
Honeymoon for Four
Honeymoon for Five
Honeymoon for Six
Honeymoon for Seven

Aloha Romance Series:
Aloha Texas
Almost Paradise
Mai Tai Marriage
Dive Into You
Look of Love
Love by Design
Love Walks In
Shell Game
Flirting with Paradise

CHAPTER ONE

Preston Sweet slammed the door of his SUV and slipped his keys into his pocket. Unlike his apartment in town, the front door of the Sweet Ranch was never locked. From the near empty drive, it looked like only his brother Carson had beat him home. Every Sunday the driveway would be filled with cars. Tonight would be the first time the house would be bursting with Sweets on a weeknight for no other reason than his mom had called and asked.

The sound of spitting gravel cut off his thoughts. Even with the dust cloud blowing in the thick summer air, preventing a clear view of the approaching car, he knew the driver had to be Rachel. His sister was the only person in the family who considered every open road a NASCAR track.

The car came to a screeching halt within a few feet of him, though it felt like inches. She probably should have moved to Hollywood and been a stunt car driver. "Cutting it pretty close, don't you think?"

Rachel yanked her overnight bag from the back seat and shook her head at her brother. "Nah. I had plenty of room."

Even though he had just seen her a couple of weeks ago, he scooped her into a warm hug as though it had been forever ago.

"Any idea what this is all about?" she mumbled into his shoulder. The same underlying tinge of tension he'd felt since his mom's cryptic call could be felt in Rachel's embrace.

He shook his head and eased back. "I can't decide if Mom announcing she's getting married would be best-case scenario or worst-case scenario."

Like a shot, Rachel sprang back. "Mom's getting married? I thought you didn't know what this is all about."

"That's not what I meant." He shook his head more forcefully. "I was simply wondering what could be so important that she would call all of us and tell us she needed us home. *Now*. Then it hit me a wedding would be something seriously important. Especially if it was *our* mother getting married again. Once my mind wandered that far, then I couldn't decide if that would be a relief or the beginning of some new kind of hell."

"She's not even dating." Rachel smacked him lightly on the arm and growled her frustration with her big brother. "Why would you even go there?"

"Because the other option was she's dying and I don't want to go there—*ever*."

On a heavy sigh, Rachel nodded. "That would certainly make getting hitched more appealing."

He reached for her bag. "Did you ever think about it?"

"Mom getting married again?"

Moving forward, he bobbed his head.

"Nope." She fell into step beside him. "I just can't picture anyone with Mom except Dad."

"Know what you mean, but still, it has to be pretty lonely some days in this big old house."

"Yeah." She stopped at the porch steps and looked up at the expanse of the beloved two-story stone and log home that had grown through the generations to house the Sweet family for well over two hundred years. "But for now, I don't think this is it."

"I hope not. I'm not ready to think about Mom remarrying. Some day, but not yet." Preston held the door open for his sister, the way his dad had drummed into all their heads since they were old enough to walk. "And the more I think about this call, the more I'm sure whatever it is, I'm not going to like it either."

"Any word from Garret?" Rachel strolled past him.

"No, and I didn't expect to hear back from our nature-loving brother. He warned us there's no cell service where he and his buddies are camping in Idaho."

"I know." His sister shrugged. "I just thought, sometimes with technology you never know."

Despite the massive appearance from the outside of the home, the inside was cozy, welcoming with large upholstered furniture that created a comfy seating area with a great view of the expansive property, and quiet. Too quiet.

Rachel paused mid-stride. "I'm surprised Mom isn't here waiting for us."

The same thing had crossed Preston's mind. For as long as he could remember, since the day he'd left home for college, the minute his mom heard the rumble of his engine, she was out the door and on the porch waving frantically at him. As a matter of fact, now that he thought about it, everything inside and out seemed unusually quiet.

"Maybe she's helping the ranch hands with something. This is around vaccine time before the big sales."

"Maybe." Without being given direction, he led his sister down the hall to the room she'd shared with her twin Jillian, and dropped the bag on the bed. "I'm going to see if I can find Carson and Mom."

"I saw a light on in the study." Rachel unzipped her bag. "I'm going to take a minute and unpack."

"Don't you usually pack a lot less?"

She shrugged. "Since I'm mostly working from home, I figured no harm in planning to stay a few extra days."

The thought to pack a bag and turn a midweek supper into a very long weekend had occurred to him as well, but then he decided that first, he had enough clothing still at the house to last him a month, and second, showing up for an extended stay might fall in the camp of overreacting to a simple call for a family dinner in the middle of the week. "That'll make Mom happy."

His sister flashed a huge toothy grin. "I know."

"Women," he muttered, laughing to himself. After four boys, and nothing but male cousins, the birth of twin girls had been a delightful surprise. That kid and his other sister had everyone in the family wrapped around their fingers from the day they were born, and he doubted that would ever change.

Retreating down the hall, he turned into his father's domain. Charles Sweet's study hadn't changed much since the days when Preston and his siblings had trotted around on wooden pony sticks with makeshift lassos and pretended to rope everything from the toy horses to the desktop lamp—and each other. In an effort to keep them all in one piece, their father had dutifully uttered the occasional warning of 'be careful' or 'not so rough'—most likely for their mother's benefit. More so though, their dad had simply done his best to get through the paperwork part of the ranch business while his children created havoc around him.

Funny, in all the time since they'd buried their father, the familiar scent of his aftershave seemed to still linger in the air. Or perhaps it was nothing more than memories and wishful thinking.

"Did Mom tell anyone why we're all here?" Carson uncapped the crystal decanter behind the desk then raised an empty glass to his brother.

"No, thanks." Preston waved off the silent invitation. "Rachel is unpacking. Neither of us has any idea what this is all about."

Carson, who since their father's passing had done his best to step up in their oldest brother Kade's absence and quietly be there for their mother, sank heavily in one of the oversized leather chairs, swirled the ice in the two fingers of bourbon, and took a long swallow.

"Looks like you've had a hard day." Preston took a seat across from him, leaving the sofa and a smaller chair for his mom and siblings.

"Hard week." Carson eyed the glass glimmering from the reflection of the nearby lamp. "Heck, more like weeks."

Hands threaded in front of him, Preston leaned forward. Even though Carson was the most private of the siblings, Preston couldn't remember seeing his brother stew so sternly over anything. "What's wrong?"

"Just another day in the flip world." Carson sighed. "Turns out the most recent project we sank all our available cash into, is now knee deep in litigation."

"That's something new."

"For me it is. Seems all the houses in that subdivision are in a class action suit against the original developers and we can't do squat until it's settled. My ninety-day rehab schedule just went down the drain."

"So now what?"

"Not sure. I'm okay for a while, but the reno budget is growing tighter every day until I come up with a plan B."

"Sorry, man." Preston changed his mind about that drink after all.

The loose board by the threshold squeaked, announcing his sister's arrival. "A little early to be drinking, isn't it?"

"What's that saying, it's five o'clock somewhere?" Carson leaned forward and set his drink on the table then looked at his watch. "It's been five o'clock on the east coast for over half an hour."

"In that case," Rachel smiled up at Preston still at the bar, "make mine on the rocks."

"Aren't you too young to drink?" Carson teased.

His sister flashed a wistful grin. "Oh, to be twenty-one again."

"Twenty-one? Aren't you sixteen?"

"Here we go again." Rachel accepted her glass and rolled her eyes at her brothers.

Didn't matter how old she grew, in their eyes she and Jillian would always be the kid sisters who needed their big bad brothers to keep them safe and out of trouble, especially since the two had been stubborn and strong-willed since birth. Not even falling from the boys' tree house and breaking an arm had taken the edge off of Rachel's adventurous streak.

"Never mind that." Preston figured the least he could do was reel in his brother's sense of humor, especially since they had more pressing matters at hand. Setting his drink aside, he slid his phone from his pocket and hit his mom's number.

"Mom?" Rachel asked.

Preston nodded, and Carson scooted to the edge of his seat, carefully watching the phone, then sliding back when the call went to voice mail.

Still staring at the now quiet phone, Rachel frowned. "Anyone else starting to feel guilty for making Mom worry when we missed curfew and forgot our phones?"

"Not me." Preston smiled. "I was perfect."

Rachel rolled her eyes at him and then her face stiffened. "Seriously, maybe we should make some phone calls. Friends, Ray, make sure she's all right."

"She's a grown woman who has worked this ranch for longer than any of us have been alive, and running it just fine without Dad. I'm sure she'll be here any minute and laugh off our concerns." Carson's words painted a picture of a calm, unconcerned son, but the look in his gaze and leaving a drink unfinished spoke volumes to just how concerned he was about their mother's tardiness. What in heaven's name could she be up to?

"Loud noise reactivity. Perceived confrontation. German Shepherd. What time?" Sarah Sue Conroy tapped the pad she'd used to scribble data on the most recent dog needing to be homed. Even with years of experience as the foster coordinator for a non-profit military canine organization, thanks to an onslaught of military working dogs recently coming through the system, her usual sources for fosters were growing slim. There had to be an answer and she'd better find it before Tuesday morning at zero nine hundred hours when this poor boy's last chance for being homed ran out. A few more details and requisite polite exchange of weather, family, and allergy season, and she disconnected the call, bringing her laptop screen to life.

"I have to run." Her father grabbed a protein bar off the counter and shoved it in his jacket pocket, then casually pilfered one, then two, of the chocolate chip cookies she'd made earlier in the day. "Mary Mahoney has finally gone into labor for real."

"Finally?" Sarah had been daughter to a country doctor

long enough, and spent enough summers playing receptionist and aide to know almost as much about medicine as her father—though every med school in the world would probably disagree with her. Still, even she knew that every pregnant woman eventually had a baby.

"She's ten days overdue and every time Braxton Hicks start she'd be in my office convinced this was *the* time."

"How do you know this isn't another false alarm?" As sure as she knew her name was Sarah Sue Conroy, she knew there would be a definitive answer.

"Heard it in her voice."

And *that* was why her dad was so very good at what he did. She still remembered the time that Mrs. Harper had called to tell the doc that she was having strong twinges and was going to climb into the tub to relax before the main event. When her husband called back an hour later in a panic, her father told him to hold the phone close to his wife's face so Sarah's father could listen. A few long moments later and the well-loved old doctor informed Mr. Harper not to wait for him, but rather to take his wife to the hospital and don't worry about the speed limits, the sheriff would understand. An hour later, Faith Harper was born.

Her father paused long enough to kiss her on the temple. "It's nice to have you back. Not much about the chaos in today's world I'm happy about, but at least one good thing has come from it. If the business world's acceptance of folks working from home means having you here instead of Austin, then it's a welcome change. Love you."

"Love you too. And it's nice to be back." In the half a dozen years since she'd moved to Austin, she hadn't realized just how much she missed living in a sleepy town. Apparently, she missed it all a lot. A whole lot of lot. Especially chatting over dinner about anything from Mildred McEntire's latest bedazzled outfit, to who'd won that day's corn hole match at the park, to the latest fight at the town council over their beloved town of Honeysuckle, Texas. Nary a week went by when there wasn't a disagreement of some kind between the faction who wanted to promote the honeysuckle arts and crafts that filled the Main Street shops with everything from candles to potpourri, and the faction who felt being corn hole capital of Texas was the bigger advantage for promotion dollars. But if her new working arrangements panned out, fingers crossed, maybe, just maybe, she could move home for good.

"Odds are I'll be home late." Her dad stood at the open front door. "First babies usually take their sweet time. If I am, you go ahead and take the casserole out of the oven and invite yourself over to the Sweets. Alice would probably enjoy the company. Even though it's been over a year, she's still a bit out of sorts over losing Charlie, not that she realizes it." He pressed his lips into a thin line and shook his head with a sigh. "Anyhow, company would do her good."

"Will do!"

The front door closed in the distance and Sarah pushed to her feet. A casserole dinner with Miss Alice would be way more fun than eating alone, waiting for her dad to come home. Besides, she hadn't seen any of the Sweets since Charlie's funeral. It was a miserable reason to come home and she'd barely had any chance to say more than "I'm sorry for your loss" to the people who had been like a second family to her for most of her life. Maybe she could even dig up a bottle of Abigail Fine's honeysuckle wine to go with dinner.

According to the oven clock, dinner would be ready in thirty minutes. Enough time for her to get a little work done. Alice Sweet had done such a great job with her son's dog, maybe she would have a few suggestions for Sarah. She'd opened a new browser and watched the swirly thing spin when another thought smacked her upside the head. Why not ask Ms. Alice if she would be willing to take on another troubled dog? After all, if she was left alone to rattle around in the big house, a new dog could be just the ticket. That is if Brady and the foster could share Alice and the house. It was the perfect solution really. Therapeutic companionship for everyone. Yes. The more she thought about it the more she was sure this would be the answer she needed. Now all she had to do was convince Alice Sweet.

CHAPTER TWO

"**O**h my. This is beautiful." Liz Klein, Alice Sweet's middle sister, lifted the item out of the box and held it up for her sister Vicki to see. Only Vicki's gaze was locked on the phone in her hand. "What's more interesting than this?"

"Alice still isn't answering her phone." Vicki looked up at her sister and smiled. "It is pretty."

"Pretty?" Liz shook her head and gingerly set the bean bag holster around her hips, snapping the front closed. "It's almost too pretty to sell."

"What?" Vicki looked up from the phone again.

Exasperated, Liz placed the custom-made holster back in the shipping box. "You'd think this was the first time our baby sister has ever not answered her phone."

"No, but she hasn't worked with the cattle since the kids were old enough to help Charlie. This is the first time she's been out working the ranch instead of one of the hands. Ever."

The way her sister emphasized *ever* gave her pause. Serious pause. "We should have closed the shop and gone to help."

Vicki shook her head. "You know she wouldn't have stood for it. This is the biggest season of the year for us with the annual championship coming up and bringing extra tourist dollars."

"About that."

Vicki tapped at her phone and grunted something that sounded similar to 'yeah.'

"We should enter this year."

"What?"

"You and I are the best corn hole players in the state and you know it."

"No. We *were* the best. Then we opened the Corn Hole Heaven and retired from competition. Conflict of interest. Now we just sell to players."

"But this is different. Alice is in a rough spot."

"I know." Vicki stared down at her phone again. "You ever get that feeling in the pit of your stomach that something just isn't quite right?"

"It's the new millennium and the world is turning upside down. I get that feeling every day."

Vicki blew out a deep and soulful sigh. "You're right. Who the heck ropes cattle and rides a horse with their cell phone in their hand?"

"While I get your drift, I doubt Alice is roping any cattle. She's probably just doing something safe like checking fence lines or feeding chickens."

"They don't have chickens."

"You know what I mean. Our sister is a lot of things, but stupid isn't one of them. She wouldn't do anything dangerous."

Vicki pressed her lips together and then blew out another sigh. "I sure do wish all the kids weren't spread out so far from home. My Luke and Chase would want to do all they could to help their aunt."

"I know, same with my boys, but if wishes were horses, beggars would ride." Liz flashed her sister a toothy grin, something she did often when quoting their Grandma Davis. "Which brings me back full circle. First prize is fifty thousand. That could go a long way to helping Alice get back on her feet."

"Yes." Vicki fingered the new holster and a sparkle lit in her eyes. "Yes, it would."

Liz's cheeks pulled back in a wide smile to rival her sister's and snapped the new holster onto her hips again. "Looks like we're going to show Mildred McEntire she's not the only one who can bedazzle the crowd."

"You'd better not mean you're going to blind me with bling."

"Of course not. That's not my style."

"Good. For a minute there, I thought I was going to have to find a new sister."

"Don't you look serious." The door closed behind their niece Jillian.

"Oh, hi sweetie." The holster still on her hips, Liz turned and drew her niece into a big bear hug. "You look prettier than an East Texas rose."

"I do take after my aunts." Jillian grinned at them. The long-running joke between the Davis women and the twins always brought a smile to their faces.

Liz undid the holster. "What brings you by? I thought y'all were going to the ranch for a family dinner."

"I am." Jill picked up a red bean bag with an embroidered American flag on it and weighed it in one hand. "I was just thinking."

Liz looked to Vicki. She didn't like the glint in her niece's eyes. Ever since the twins learned to speak, they could get their aunts to do or say anything. Right about now, say was the problem.

"Mama tells y'all absolutely everything."

Uh-oh. With there being nothing but boys in the family until Jill and Rachel were born, it was plum easy for every adult in the family to cave in to the blonde pigtails and sweet smiles. Even if they didn't wear pigtails anymore, resistance was futile. Except this time their sister had sworn them to secrecy.

"I don't know about everything," Vicki offered up quickly. They needed to stay strong—and silent.

"But enough?" Jillian dropped the bean bag back in the display bowl, then inched closer. "Something is going on with Mom and I'd like to know what it is."

"Something's very wrong." Preston stomped the dust free from his boots and strode across the kitchen. "The bunkhouse is empty. No sign of Ray or any of the other hands."

Carson sprang to his feet. "What do you mean no sign of?"

"No clothes, no equipment, nothing. Except for one bunk."

"That does it." Rachel reached for the phone. "I'm calling the sheriff."

"You do realize," Jillian held up a hand, "I couldn't get a word out of Aunt Liz and Aunt Vicki. I admit they looked a little nervous, but you know neither one of them has ever been able to keep a secret."

"At least not from us," Rachel added.

"So, if Mom has whatever is going on under control, she is not going to like us bringing in the sheriff."

Preston pinched the bridge of his nose. "No, but all this is simply—"

A scratching at the back door, followed by a single woof had everyone turning their heads toward the sounds.

"Brady," a couple of voices muttered.

Another bark and the siblings already on their feet sprinted to the door.

Brady seemed to focus directly on Preston, maybe because he was the brother who looked the most like Kade, or maybe he was simply the closest to the door, but the dog let out a single woof and doubled around, hurrying away from the house.

"I guess we're following the dog." Preston raised his hands and quickly dropped them to his sides.

Jillian muttered, "We don't have any wells." The teasing reference to Lassie and Timmy falling down the well fell flat on most of them. Especially once they one by one realized the dog was now galloping at full speed and there was no way they were going to keep up on foot.

"I'll get the four-wheeler," Rachel shouted over her shoulder.

Carson shook his head. "Jeep would be better. Then we can all ride together."

Jillian stopped in her tracks. "I'll stay put. At least one of us should be here in case that dog isn't taking us to Mom and only leading us on a wild goose chase to a stash of buried dog treasures."

"Good idea." Preston did his best to sound calm and collected and hide the fear from his voice. Right about now, none of this looked good to him.

A few minutes more and the dog barked again, this time doing an impatient-with-them dance in place, and once again bolting across the field when the Jeep appeared ready to follow his lead.

Rachel shook her head. "I swear that dog is definitely directing us somewhere and none too happy that it's taken us this long to follow."

Preston's first thought was it better not be a treasure trove of dog bones, but his second thought kicked that aside—hard. If it wasn't bones, then it would be his mother, and if she needed to send the dog out with an SOS, wherever she was, couldn't be good.

As his speed demon sister drove them over the uneven terrain, the backseat of the Jeep sent him nearly airborne again. If he wasn't careful, the next bump might just send him flying off the back end and the poor dog would have to do search and rescue.

"There!" Preston pointed ahead to a big blur of a horse on the horizon. "Blaze is just standing."

"Then Mom should be nearby." Except the dog wasn't running toward the horse, the animal ran at a diagonal. He was heading toward the fence line between their land and Doc Conroy's property. Preston didn't think he'd ever hear himself say this while his sister Rachel was at the wheel, but never say never: "Gun it."

Carson yelled over the roar of the engine. "When the dog stops, slow the hell down. We don't want to run Mom over."

There. Someone had finally said it out loud. None of them expected to find their mother picking flowers. In what seemed like only a heartbeat of time, the dog stopped at the fence line and Rachel eased her foot from the gas pedal. The closer they got, the tighter the knots in his stomach twisted. He couldn't quite make out what the dog was doing, and then he heard a collective gasp at the same time he figured out what Brady was up to. Ever so gingerly, the dog that had lived at their mother's side since retiring out of the military, inched his way left and right, carefully sniffing from head to toe at their mother tangled in the barbed wire fence.

"Oh, hell," Rachel muttered. She'd barely come to a stop when both he and Carson had bolted out of the Jeep.

Half a step away, Preston stopped and grabbed the tool bag from under the seat.

"I'll get the first aid kit." Rachel leaned over the other side. Ranch vehicles were often a combination of tool shed and doc's office. Just enough equipment to patch something or someone up until later.

"Took you…" their mom sucked in a low breath, "long enough."

Not only was she able to talk, she was able to tease. Like a hot spring on a cool day, relief bathed over every tense muscle. Except the closer Preston got to the fence line and the more clearly his mother's predicament came into view, tension once again had a stranglehold on him. One leg up and tucked under a run of wire, her other leg rested in the opposite direction, the barbed spikes tearing into her jeans. A nasty gash cut into one arm. With the weight of her torso pushing down on the fence, she resembled a wishbone on Thanksgiving Day. It wouldn't take much effort to snap her in two. With every passing moment, more trickles of blood appeared where the spikes had shredded bits of fabric and cut into her skin. Carson cast a sideways glance in his direction, and Preston barely nodded in response. This was not going to be easy. At least, unlike an entrapped cow, his mother would know not to move when they started to cut her free. The trick would be avoiding any more injuries.

"Dare I ask what the hell happened?" Rachel's tone may have been strong, but the worried look in her eyes sharpened when her gaze fell on the blood-soaked sleeve.

Careful not to move, her mom spoke softly. "Rattler got too close."

That was all they needed. Bad enough their mother was trapped in cutting barbed wire, a snake bite on top of that would have been too much.

Preston had the tool bag open at his mother's feet. "Did he bite you?"

Wincing, his mom shook her head slightly. "Spooked Blaze. Someone better check and see if he got bit. I don't want to lose that horse."

Rachel set the first aid kit at her brother's side. "I'll run over and check."

While his sister trotted over to where the horse stood, Preston squatted by his mom's left leg. "I'm going to cut you lose so that you can put some weight on that leg."

"And I'm going to put my arm under your middle and try to keep the pressure from shifting on the wires," Carson added.

"You be careful now," she told her son in the same commanding voice she used on them as children about to get into mischief. "Don't need you all cut up too."

"Yes, ma'am."

Sucking in a fortifying breath, Preston snipped at the first wire, carefully helping to support his mom's leg with his other hand. Two more snips and the foot was untangled and on the ground. The sound of Blaze's heavy hoofs thundered in his ears. Didn't matter what kind of horsepower it was, Rachel simply didn't do slow.

"No harm done, and no sign of that rattling rascal." Rachel slid off the horse, and dropped the reins to ground tie her mom's horse, then hurried back to her side.

A few more snips and their mother was free and actually smiled at them. Preston already had his handkerchief pressed against the gash on his mother's arm, and without a word, his sister added packing and quickly wrapped the wound.

Cut up from her forehead to her ankles, the woman had spent at least an hour stuck on biting barbed wire and yet here she stood wobbly but smiling at them. "I admit I wasn't looking forward to spending the night on that torture chamber until y'all figured out where I was."

"I don't even want to think about how this could have turned out if we hadn't been at the house looking for you."

Preston tossed the wire cutters into the bag and debated if he dared lift his mother to carry her to the car.

"Forget about it, Preston Sweet. I can see what you're thinking and the answer is no. I can walk." Their mom leaned over to scratch Brady's ears and almost fell over. No water in this Texas heat, a bloody gash, and trickling wounds, she had to be dangerously weak.

"Easy, Mom." Rachel lurched forward, grabbing hold of her mother's arm to steady her and sucked in a deep breath when her mom winced at the maneuver. "Sorry."

"No problem." Except she moved to take a step toward the Jeep and almost went down again.

"Sorry Mom, this may hurt." Preston leaned against his mother's less injured side, carefully slid an arm under her legs and eased her up. "We need to get you to the doc's."

"Not necessary. A little antiseptic here and there and after a good night's sleep, I'll be fine."

"Mother." Carson shadowed the pair. "Don't be difficult."

Rachel grabbed hold of the horse's reins. "I'll ride Blaze and meet you back at the house. But this time I agree with these two. You need to have those cuts and that foot looked at."

"Better add her wrist." Carson nudged his chin in her direction.

Preston had been so concerned with the cuts and new bruises that were beginning to show up that he hadn't even noticed the changing color on her wrist and that it was nearly twice the size of what it should be.

His mom followed his gaze and waved him off. "I may have twisted it pulling on the reins. I managed to stay in the saddle the first time Blaze reared up, but by the time he'd worked up a good strong panic and reared up again, not only couldn't I hang on, I bounced against him before he tossed me several feet."

"Right onto the fence," Preston spoke through clenched teeth and pulled his phone from his pocket. "If you won't go to the doctor, then the doc will just have to come to you."

His mom lightly rubbed her swollen wrist with her good hand. Just about the only part of her that had been spared a biting kiss from the wire fence. "I suppose it will be fine if it keeps you two from hovering like overzealous boy scouts."

Brady hopped into the Jeep as Carson started the engine, and sat guard over his mistress. Either too tired, or in too much pain, his mom merely smiled at the large German Shepherd. "I knew I could count on you."

As soon as Preston was sure his mother was taken care of, that dog was getting the biggest steak he'd ever seen. "Man's best friend."

"Isn't that the truth?" Carson's grip on the steering wheel tightened. "Who knows how long before we would have found you without Brady."

An image of finding his mother days later flashed through his mind. Maybe the dog would get steak for the rest of his life.

CHAPTER THREE

Deep in the numbers for her latest foster project, the unexpected ringing of the old kitchen landline startled Sarah out of her thoughts. Springing up, she trotted to the other room, too late to answer. Halfway back to the sofa, the phone rang again.

This time she darted back more quickly. "Hello."

"Uh…" A quiet moment passed. "I'm sorry. I thought I was dialing the doc's number."

"You are, but he's not here at the moment."

"Sarah Sue?"

"Yes."

"It's Preston. Preston Sweet."

"Oh, hi." She hadn't recognized the voice at first, but now she did. All the Sweets had a deep soothing timbre that made a person want to sit back and listen to them read a phone book.

"There's been a little accident."

From his tone she couldn't tell how serious.

"Little?"

"Mom fell off a horse." She could hear Carson mutter from somewhere nearby.

"I did not fall!" his mother hollered from within earshot of the phone.

Sarah chuckled softly. If not for the reassuring sound of Alice Sweet's irritated voice, the words *Mom fell off a horse* would have sent chills down her spine. "I see your mom hasn't changed much since I left town. Plenty of sass."

"No," he chuckled too, "afraid not."

"I was thrown," his mom continued. "And by one of the best."

"Thrown?" She didn't need to be a doctor for a list of potential internal injuries to run through her mind, along with memories of every time her father had grumbled over a simple injury going south from unexpected complications. "How bad is she hurt?"

"Not really sure. She's conscious—and sassy—so I'm assuming that's a good sign, but I'm an accountant, what do I know about broken people."

His choice of words wasn't at all reassuring. She wanted to know how broken was broken.

"She won't come to your father. We're heading back to the house now and need your dad to please come check her out. There was no answer at his office. Is he home yet?"

"Afraid not. The Mahoney baby thought today would be a good day to arrive." At least she hoped it was going to be today. And soon, if not already. She reached into her pocket. "Hold on, I'll text him and see how much longer this baby is going to take to make an appearance."

"Thanks. Normally, I wouldn't want to interrupt a man delivering a baby, but I think having someone who knows more than spreadsheets and profit statements to look for broken bones, things none of us know to look for, and stitch her up would be a good idea."

"Stitch her up? Where'd she fall?"

"On the fence line."

He didn't have to say anything else. Her family weren't cattle ranchers, but she'd grown up next door to them and knew exactly what falling on a fence meant—barbed wire. She really, really hoped that Mrs. Mahoney's baby was in a hurry to arrive.

"Easy, Carson," Preston snapped. Sarah had never heard him speak so sharply. "Sorry. The Jeep hit an uneven patch of dirt and Mom winced."

She could hear Carson barking back, *I'm going as easy as I can and still get us home in one piece before the next millennium.* Growing up, she'd spent as much time at the Sweet house as she had her own, especially after her mom passed. She knew the whole family well enough to recognize things had to be worse than Preston was letting on if both brothers were losing their cool. Normally she would have texted her dad as she'd said, but this was important. If he was too busy to answer, he would let it go to voice mail.

One ring and her father picked up. "Doc here."

She sure hoped that meant he was finishing up. "Dad, how's it going?"

"Seems we've got more time than we thought."

Not what she'd wanted to hear. Talking as fast as she could, she shared what little info she had and then picked the handset up off the counter. "I'm sorry. Mrs. Mahoney is still only six centimeters. It's likely going to be a while."

Preston didn't have to say anything for her to know that wasn't what they wanted her to report any more than she'd wanted to hear it. "Got it," he muttered.

"Can I do anything to help?" Heaven knew what she could do. The last few years of her life had been spent with mostly four-legged friends.

"I hoped you'd say that. We'll be at the house in about five minutes."

"On my way." She wasn't her father, but she could at least grab some extra first aid products just in case. Hurrying around her dad's office, she tossed everything and anything that made sense into a bag and bolted out the front door. The entire distance from her door to the Sweets she said her prayers. If Ms. Alice was in as bad shape as it sounded from Preston, there was one thing Sarah could be sure of: she knew just enough about medicine to know that most likely under these circumstances, she wouldn't know nearly enough.

From the second they pulled up in front of the house, everything seemed to happen in high speed. Jillian stood at the front door, her expression grim and anxious. Carson and Preston shot orders back and forth on the most efficient way to get their mom upstairs, and every time their mother winced in pain, Brady looked at the two brothers and growled softly under his breath. Neither feared he would hurt them, but the pup was making it very clear he wanted them to be more careful with his mistress. They'd barely gotten their mother out of the Jeep when Sarah Sue's car could be heard crunching the driveway gravel beneath its tires.

Parked and out the door like a shot, she hurried to the porch and followed everyone inside. "I came right over. How ya doin', Ms. Alice?"

"I've had… better days." Preston's mom tried to smile, but it wasn't quite working. She hadn't said much in the short ride back to the house; only not till this moment did he consider her silence wasn't a mere lack of something to say but a sign she'd grown weaker.

From the sideways glance Sarah tossed in his direction, clearly she was thinking the same thing.

"Where we going?" Sarah looked to Jillian at the head of the line.

"Her room," three voices echoed.

They'd inched their way to the upstairs room and paused at the foot of the bed.

"How are we going to do this?" Carson asked.

"We have to clean the wounds on her back." Jillian stood at the head of the bed.

While all the others mutely stared at their sister, as if unsure what to do next, Sarah focused on their mom. "Maybe set her down on her right side, then Jillian and I can clean the wounds. By then she might be more comfortable on her tummy."

All heads bobbed, but Preston was worried about the blood-soaked bandage on his mom's arm. "I'm not a doctor but I'm afraid that arm is going to need stitches."

Sarah nodded. "Might, but based on when Ms. Alice thinks she fell, we've got maybe twenty more hours."

"What do you mean?" At her mom's side, Jillian stood with her nose crinkled.

"After twenty-four hours it's too late to stitch up a wound. So, let's get her out of these clothes. We'll need a good pair of scissors."

"These are my favorite jeans!" his mom exclaimed with more energy than she'd showed all evening.

"Trust me," Sarah smiled, "cutting them off will be much easier on you."

"That's what you think," the head of the Sweet family muttered and rolled ever so slightly on her side until she looked to be as comfortable as she was going to get.

Scissors in hand, Sarah looked up at Carson and Preston. "You two just going to stand there?"

"Oh." Preston took a step in retreat. "I guess we'll wait outside."

Carson nodded and followed his brother into the hall.

Preston leaned his head back against the wall. "Any of us have spent enough time on this ranch to know how to do basic doctoring."

"Yeah." Carson nodded. "But none of those animals were our mother."

"Exactly."

"What are y'all doing lined up like first graders waiting for the restroom?" Rachel came strutting down the hall.

"Jill and Sarah are stripping Mom to treat the wounds."

Rachel nodded. Her hand on the doorknob, she turned the handle and pushed her way inside.

From where they stood they could hear their mother hollering through the once again closed door, "What is this, a sideshow?"

"You know she's going to be just fine," Carson said over Preston's shoulder.

"I know." He nodded. "But she scared the hell out of me."

A set of soft footfalls made their way up the hall. Preston lifted his gaze to meet the approaching ranch hand. An unfamiliar face. It had been ages since he'd spent enough time on the ranch to know all the hands by name. Of course he knew Ray. They all did. Ray had been foreman under his father and knew every inch of the operation as well as their dad. Preston couldn't begin to imagine how they would have made it through the most difficult days after Charlie Sweet's unexpected death if not for Ray. He'd seamlessly stepped into the role their dad had filled, saving the ranch and the family.

Hat in hand, the stranger's eyes scanned each of them. Only the tick in his jaw showed his unease with finding Alice Sweet's sons standing in the hall.

"Mom had a little accident." Carson answered the unasked question.

"Accident?" The man pressed his lips tightly together.

Preston pushed away from the wall. "She was tossed from her horse. Landed on the fence. Nothing seems to be broken, but she's pretty cut up."

Fingering the hat in his hand, the man's lips pulled tightly together as his gaze shifted to the closed door. "Doc with her?"

Preston shook his head. "Sarah Sue, the doc's daughter, is tending to her."

"I see." His gaze shifted briefly to the door then back. "I'd best be getting back to the bunkhouse. I'll check in on Ms. Sweet in the morning. Please tell her I went out to the farthest pasture as she asked. Fixed some fence line while I was there, but there's more to do. A lot more."

"Where's Ray?" Preston asked.

"And the others?" Carson added.

The man slapped his hat against his leg and for a split second Preston thought he might spit before speaking. "Ms. Sweet had better explain that."

The door behind him finally swung open and all of Preston's questions for this man slipped away. The time waiting in the hall had seemed like forever. He blew out a relieved sigh, no longer concerned with the footsteps of the departing ranch hand.

Rachel stood in the doorway. "Mom's all cleaned up and resting, but she still wants to talk to everyone. Sarah says we'd better hurry. She only gave Mom some ibuprofen for the discomfort, but she thinks Mom's going to give out sooner than later."

For everyone's sake, Preston hoped all his mother wanted was to once again thank them for finding her, because whatever the reason she'd called them all together, he wasn't up for any more surprises tonight.

CHAPTER FOUR

The four siblings lined up along the edges of the bed. Head bowed, gaze lowered, Sarah took a step back.

To Alice, the simple effort of clearing her throat seemed gargantuan. She knew the pills she'd taken were beginning to kick in. Under normal circumstances, it would take a dose of medicine suitable for a Clydesdale to knock her out, but her body had been through too much in the last few days, and the last few hours had completely pushed her already tired body over the edge. She suspected a soft breeze could have knocked her over. Another concentrated effort and she successfully cleared her throat, and then sighed. "This isn't easy for me."

"You don't have to talk, Mom." Jill patted her mother's good hand.

Just the idea of her not wanting to speak made her chuckle. The sharp ensuing pain that shot in several directions at once smothered the smile and made her wince. She'd have to be more careful. "That'll be the day when I'm too tired—or weak—to talk."

This time it was Preston who smothered a hint of amusement. Concern lingered in those big steel blue eyes, but her last crack seemed to have assuaged at least a hint of her children's worry.

"We've got some big problems with the ranch."

Sarah eased back another step. "I should probably—"

"No." Alice waved her back into the fold. "You've practically been one of the family since you were old enough to stand. Besides, the town's going to find out sooner or later when they notice all my ranch hands but one are gone."

Alice Sweet blinked, drawing on every ounce of strength she had. The previous week she'd spent day and night poring over the books. Checking not once, not twice, but over and over. The paperwork, the bank accounts, her husband's personal memos. None of it had been good. Along the way, she'd had more than one heart to heart with the Lord *and* her deceased husband.

"You're telling us Ray is gone?" Her son's voice carried the same incredulous tone that had settled in her own mind as she'd considered the facts. The interminable drought had given Alice the first real challenge in running the ranch since Charlie had died. Had that been the only challenge she'd have handled it, but the books had shown that wasn't the case. The ranch was bleeding cherry red ink, and if she screwed up her next move, she could lose it all.

Eyes closed, Alice could still see the new ranch hand standing yesterday at her back door looking more chagrined than a little boy tasked with picking out his own switch.

His words had come out especially slow and smooth, even for a West Texas cowboy. "I'm not sure how to say this so I'll just say it straight out. Got back from the line shack a little bit ago. Found the bunk house empty of folks. No surprise at this hour of the day, exceptin' all the gear is gone too. Not a boot, belt, or pair of britches in the place."

She hadn't liked the sudden souring of her stomach contents. All the pieces she'd been uncovering the last few days were falling into place more and more and she wasn't liking the picture she was seeing.

"Ma'am. I've, uh, well, I've been thinking lately something around here was off. It's why I was checking the herds in the far pastures. I don't mean to overstep my place, but I think you've got more trouble on your hands than just an unhappy crew moving on to greener pastures."

Even more than twenty-four hours later, what she was about to say was the part Alice hadn't wanted to believe. Had prayed she'd been wrong about, and wanted desperately to will away. "Seems our trusted foreman's been cooking the books."

Shock, surprise, and concern took over each of the

siblings faces.

Carson was the first to speak. "How bad?"

Alice swallowed hard, still asking herself how could she have let this happen. "All the male calves that were going to give us the cash infusion to help ride through the hard times are gone."

"What do you mean gone?" Preston had inched closer to the bed.

"You name it. Everything from stillborns to pneumonia. Even lost a few with their mamas in that last flash flood." Or at least that's what she'd been told with this crazy feast or famine Texas weather.

Shock still reflected in her eyes, Jill grabbed hold of the brass footboard. "Really?"

Alice hated the pained look on her children's faces as much as she hated how she'd failed them. "That's what Ray led me to believe. According to the records, not one of the live births has made it to market."

"I sense a *but* coming." Preston moved in next to Jill.

"Got a call from Sean Farraday, one of Charlie's ranching buddies in West Texas. Long story short, there was an oddity in this year's sale of calves, so rather than wait for Ray to call him back, he reached out to me."

"So there *are* calves to sell?" A relieved grin slid across Rachel's face.

"Ray's been selling off cattle and recording it as animal loss. I've had more stolen and dead cattle this year than made any sense. Until now. Most of the wood and supplies your dad bought for the new calving barn are gone too. Probably sold. So even if we wanted to finish that project..." her words trailed off.

"Oh, crud." Preston raked his fingers through his hair. "Are you sure? That it's Ray?"

She nodded. "I called the sheriff yesterday morning. He was across the county, told me not to talk to Ray, to stay put until he could get here."

"So Ray's in jail?"

"Afraid not." The whole thing had been insane. Her sister Vicki had hurried over as soon as Alice called with the bad news, determined to keep her company until the sheriff arrived while their other sister Liz stayed in town to mind the shop. Sitting side by side at the kitchen table, when Alice finally finished updating her sister on all the ugly details she'd learned, her eyes wide like a startled screeching owl, Vicki snapped her mouth shut and then sighed. Together they'd waited, doing a miserable job at reining in their imaginations. When someone rapped on the back door, the pair had almost jumped out of their skins, unsure if it was the sheriff or the thieving foreman.

The only calm one in the room had been Brady. On the floor, positioned the same as every day, her son's German Shepherd was in the perfect spot to lunge at any unwelcome intruder. One brow slightly raised, the dog barely lifted his gaze to the door, but refrained from moving another muscle. If the visitor passed muster with the best friend her son's military buddies had ever loved, then she could turn off her spooked alarm. Through the glass door, she recognized a ranch hand who'd been hired on a few months previously, though at the time she couldn't remember his name. Hiring and firing had been another thing she probably shouldn't have let Ray handle.

Now in her bedroom, Carson had moved to stand beside his brother. The kids probably didn't realize it but they were closing ranks, coming together to deal with whatever situation life threw at them. "If Ray's not in jail, then where is he?"

Wouldn't she like to know. Apparently, Ray and all her ranch hands, except Clint, had not only colluded to rob her blind, they'd taken off before the sheriff could be brought in, leaving her with an unholy mess. *Oh, Charlie. What are we going to do?*

One by one, the next generation of Sweets walked out of their mother's room in single file.

"I want to see the books." Already marching down the

hall, Carson clenched and unclenched his hands. "Then I have a few questions for this Clint guy. Starting with, where the hell was he when Mom was falling off a horse?"

It wasn't really a question, but it was exactly what Preston was thinking. He needed to see the ranch records. All of them.

Funny how no one needed to say a word, but they all proceeded directly to the study.

"I think this calls for a drink." Rachel crossed the room and opening the small fridge, pulled out a bottle of white wine. "Who's joining me?"

"Make mine a bourbon." Carson settled in by the computer.

A few feet behind him, Jillian followed her brother into the room. "I can't believe all of this is happening at once."

"I'd better call Dad and give him an update." Sarah's eyes widened. "I mean on her condition, not the, uhm, other things."

Preston settled himself behind his brother. Impatient, he nudged Carson aside. "You may be the king of flipping property, but spreadsheets are my domain."

Carson stood and waved at the screen. "It's all yours, brother."

It didn't take long for Preston to confirm everything their mother had told them. "The ranch is in some serious trouble. If Dad hadn't chosen the year he died to borrow against the land to upgrade the hay equipment, build a new calving barn, or if the drought hadn't struck just when we needed to increase hay production to pay for the upgrades, maybe we could have survived the only person we all trusted to run the ranch, beside Mom and Dad, stabbing us in the back instead. But all three has created the perfect storm for catastrophe."

"How much money is it going to take?" Jill set her untouched wine glass down. "To get us over the hump? I mean, the candle shop had a good tourist season and with the corn hole championship coming up and the uptick in online orders, this is looking to be my best year ever, so I'm glad to contribute, but we're not talking about my bank account looking anything like Fort Knox."

He almost didn't have the heart to tell them, but he had no choice. "Hay balers and new tractors, those alone set Dad back half a million."

Carson looked hopeful. "Then we can sell it and pay down the loan."

"According to the books, we bought the equipment but then there's also a fire loss recorded."

"Translation." Carson sighed. "Ray probably sold it."

Preston pinched the bridge of his nose before facing his brother again. "That's my guess. Just to stop the snowballing penalties and interest, we'll need almost a hundred k to cover the back payments that haven't been made."

"Ray?" Rachel's eyes did that scared owl imitation.

Preston nodded. "Then there's not enough hay to get what few cows we have left through winter. So that'll be—"

"More money," Carson muttered.

"Yeah," Preston agreed. And that was only the beginning of the list.

Sarah Sue strolled into the room. "Dad says that he's expecting the newest Mahoney to be here soon and then he's going to stop in on his way home, so no one shoot him if you hear the front door opening in the middle of the night."

The comment was meant to lighten the mood, but the forced smiles around the room all resembled nervous tics.

Rachel leaned forward in her chair. "What are the chances of talking the Honeysuckle Bank into giving us a loan against the trust?"

"Ha." Jill shook her head. "Does slim to none sound familiar?"

"She's right." Carson leaned back, tapping his fingers on the edge of the sofa. "Whole reason our beloved, however many great-grandfathers ago set the thing up with a bank and not a family member was so that it would be guaranteed to last through the generations."

"Well," Preston continued to scroll through different documents, "you have to give the old goat credit for getting it right. There's plenty of money there. We just can't touch it."

"Wait a minute." Sarah Sue looked to Preston. "Y'all are trust fund babies?"

This time Rachel laughed out loud. "Not hardly, but every Sweet since Grover Eugene Sweet has inherited a small percent of the trust upon their first wedding anniversary."

"Really?" Sarah frowned.

"Really," Carson confirmed.

"Wow. Sounds more like a ridiculous plot for an old MGM musical."

"Or the beginnings of a film noir," Jill added.

Carson nodded. "It's my understanding that there's a small up front payment after the, er, honeymoon, followed by a nice little monthly supplement the first year of marriage, but the big payoff is the first anniversary. Once everyone in the current generation is married, then the principle isn't touched again until the next one starts to marry."

"And this has been going on for how long?" Sarah asked.

Carson shrugged, brows crinkled in thought. Jill stared at the ceiling doing math in her head, but it was Preston who replied, "Started six generations back. Originating in 1837."

"Almost two hundred years?" Sarah Sue looked as stunned over that news as the rest of them were over their current situation. The Sweet family ranch had been a solid operation since before any of them were born.

"Like I said," Carson took a slow sip of his bourbon, "it's a nice sum."

Rachel leaned forward again. "As in enough to get us out of this jam?"

"Don't bother going there." Carson faced his sister. "The bank will never agree to a loan."

"Maybe not." Rachel actually cracked a smile. "But they'd have to payout for a wedding."

Jill rolled her eyes skyward. "Someone give the girl a

cola. That glass of wine has gone straight to her head."

"No it hasn't and you know it." Like a cat ready to pounce, Rachel scooted to the edge of her seat, rocking on the balls of her feet. "Think about it. All we need to do in order to bail the ranch out of the immediate threat is for one of us to get married. And fast."

CHAPTER FIVE

"**S**eriously. Someone take her wine away." Jill waved her arms in frustration at her sister. The gesture reminding Sarah of when they were all kids and Jill and her twin would have completely opposing ideas. They may have been born minutes apart on the same day but the similarities ended there.

"Think about it." Rachel pushed to her feet and approached her sister. "Foreigners do it all the time for a green card, except they have to stay married for two years, not one."

For a split second, Sarah wondered if she'd fallen and bumped her head and didn't remember. A subdural hematoma or concussion would explain this bizarre conversation. And of all the crazy ideas that her best friends had ever had, this one was a doozy.

Up on her feet, Jill waved a hand at her sister and grabbed a bag of nuts from the bar. "Don't you think if falling in love were that easy, we'd all be married by now?"

"Unless it's a business arrangement." Carson took another sip of his drink.

"Not you too!" Jill threw her arms up in the air and spun around on her heel before collapsing onto the sofa.

"This isn't a new concept. Television executives got rich making instant marriage reality TV shows, and modern day international mail order brides are big business."

"Time out." Jill set her drink on the table and sucked in a long breath. "I'm not saying I agree with any of this, but even if it were possible for one of us to find a person to marry on short notice, Mom would never let us do it. Not even to save the ranch."

"She's right," Preston spoke up.

"Finally. Someone with sense in the room." Jill's arms cut through the air again.

"Then don't tell her." Carson set his half-full drink aside and leaning forward, resting his arms on his thighs, steepled his fingers together. "I've got all my credit tied up in our current deal that has ground to a halt for who knows how long. I might be able to borrow a little more, but it wouldn't be anywhere near enough to tide us over for an entire year and the interest would just dig us deeper in the hole. As it is, according to those numbers we're going to need to do a lot of fast thinking to undo this mess. I, for one, cannot imagine not having the only home we've ever known sold to the highest bidder."

Hear, hear, multiple voices chorused. Even Sarah knew, for all of them, the ranch was more than a house, or business—it was who the Sweets had been for hundreds of years.

"Well," Carson continued, "one of us getting married would be just the start, but at least it's a start."

"I know this isn't my place." Sarah still couldn't believe how badly things had turned for the Sweets. "I don't have a whole lot of savings, but I have a bit and heaven knows I'm earning next to nothing in interest. I'd be glad to make a neighborly loan."

A smile tipped the corners of Preston's mouth upward. "That's very nice of you, but Mom would really blow a gasket if we took your savings."

"Well, one thing is for sure." Carson lifted a single finger. "With our busiest season upon us and no help, looks like while I'm waiting for the green light to move forward with my current project, I'll be moving back to the ranch and getting reacquainted with a little hard labor."

Preston rubbed the back of his neck with one hand and then just let his elbow hang. "I'll do the same. I can work remotely from anywhere. I'll just do ranching at the crack of dawn and my accounting work after lunch into the evening."

"I don't have to be at the store till ten." Jill sighed. "I

can put in a few hours here. That is if I move into our old room again."

"You mean *we*." Rachel smiled at her sister. "I'm only doing field work two days a week. The rest of the time I'm working from home. Thankfully, social services is happy to save money not heating and cooling a big building. I can put in my share of hard labor, but we'll still be short hands and we'll still need a huge chunk of change to stop any more losses."

"You might as well say it." Preston blinked hard. "To stop us from losing the ranch."

Rachel nodded. "Exactly. Which, if I'm reading the writing on the wall correctly, brings us full circle to not just one of us, but we all have to try and find someone to marry us. That will increase the odds of us having our inheritance sooner than later."

Jill pressed her lips tightly together. Sarah couldn't tell if she was growing angrier or coming around to her siblings' way of thinking. Either way the whole thing seemed crazy surreal. How did a ranch that had been around for over two hundred years, with a nice normal happy family, suddenly find themselves facing a life suitable for a reality TV show?

Slowly, Jill let out a long, deep sigh. "I'm not saying I agree with any of this, but if I were to go along, where are we supposed to find these marital prospects? Ones that will fool Mom, because you know she's not going to let us do it for the money, and she's not going to believe that any of us, never mind *all of us*, have met someone and fallen head over heels in love in a week."

The siblings had gone from taking turns communicating to speaking on top of one another and growing louder and louder. Jill was still the only one with viable objections, from what's in it for the spouse, to sex, to the cost of community property. For someone who saw the worst side of society at her day job, Rachel seemed surprisingly willing to scour the internet for a prospect with little concern for the risks. Carson clearly was stuck in litigation mode because he continued to harp on the need for prenups and clarity before moving forward with this, and Sarah couldn't begin to imagine what Garret and Kade would have to say when they found out.

The whole time, Sarah kept her focus on Preston. He'd had the least to say and the most intense look on his face. Normally deep blue eyes had teetered on shades of stormy gray as soon as he'd sat down by the computer. She'd love to know exactly what was going through that complicated brain of his. Though she could venture a guess that already he was calculating a way to make this work without leaving collateral damage, and as one of the siblings had mentioned, when you involve human emotions there's usually collateral damage when a relationship—no matter how platonic—ends.

She very much wanted to help her neighbors, but she especially wished she could run her thumb across the deep-set lines creating ridges in Preston's forehead and make all his worries go away. And wasn't that just ridiculous. If anything, as a kid, Preston had been the one to watch out for her and his younger sisters, not the other way around.

The voices got louder and deeper, and Preston remained silent on the sidelines. She and Preston were the only two who hadn't even tried to get a word in edgewise for the last twenty minutes. Growing up, she always felt she understood Preston better than his brothers. Didn't hurt any that he'd held a soft spot in her heart since she was six years old, fell off the rope swing, and splashed in the storm-high creek. She'd been more scared than in danger, but at only ten years old, Preston had been the one to dive in and rescue her. Her first experience with a knight in shining armor. Now, she could almost feel the turmoil churning inside of him and wished she could do something, anything, to make this all better. *Anything.* That one word rattled around in her thoughts and like a sudden bolt of lightning, the idea struck her.

"Excuse me." Sarah's politeness fell on deaf ears. "Hey y'all," she shouted a bit louder.

Preston's gaze met hers, and with the cutest little smile, he stuck his fingers in the edge of his mouth and let out an ear-piercing sound. When the room fell silent, his smile grew and he waved his arm in her direction, giving her the floor.

Still looking out for her, his assist made her smile. She turned to face the siblings. "I think I can help."

Preston shook his head. "We already said we can't take your money."

She sucked in a breath, crossed the room, stood toe to toe with Preston, and chin up, leveled her gaze with his. "Then take me."

Preston blinked—twice. He had to have heard Sarah wrong, and if he hadn't, there had to be a much more sensible understanding of her words than the thoughts ricocheting in his overactive imagination.

"Excuse me?" From the expression on everyone's face, Jill had just spoken for all the Sweets.

"Okay. Maybe that didn't come out right. What I mean is if one of you needs to marry in a hurry, needs someone willing to go along with this charade—because it is a charade—for a whole year, and make it believable to your mom and the town and bank, then it makes sense for one of you to fall for a friend."

Rachel bobbed her head. "Friends to lovers *is* a common trope in romance novels."

"Trope?" Carson looked at his sister as if she'd just announced she was marrying an alien.

"Common premise in popular books," Preston explained. "Like innocent wrongly accused."

"Ah." Carson nodded. "Makes sense."

Sarah nodded at Preston for the correct explanation. "According to town gossip through the years, Jill had one foot in the church when she dated Bobby Prescott, but then she smartened up and since Bobby's wife is pregnant with baby number four, he's not a good candidate for this plan."

"Dodged a bullet there," Jill muttered.

"And Carson, you've made discretion an art form. If you've ever hooked up with anyone in this town, it's the biggest secret since what happened to Jimmy Hoffa."

Carson lifted one side of his mouth into a mischievous grin and Preston could almost see Sarah considering just how many secrets did their brother have.

"Unless I can convince Jimmy Henderson to leave sunny California, which I doubt will happen since he swore never to set foot in this God-forsaken town again," Rachel sighed, "then I'll probably have to start from scratch too."

"Which leaves us," Preston spoke softly as if that would make what he had to say less jarring, less absurd.

They'd never been an item. Not even close, but ever since her senior prom, the idea had been in everyone else's mind. A handful of chaperones had mentioned what a lovely couple they made. Of course they probably said that to every one of the kids. His mom had gone out of her way to point out what a nice girl Sarah was. How well she fit into the family. Except she was just finishing high school and he was about to move onto his first full-time job.

Shifting her gaze from her brother to Sarah and back again, Jill shook her head. "You two are really considering this, aren't you?"

"It could work." Preston shrugged, unsure of who he was trying to convince. "There'd have to be a little juggling and finessing, but we could probably buy some time on a few of the debts, enough to get the first monthly allowance."

"Will it be enough?" Carson asked.

"A stop gap. We'll need to put all ranch earnings back into the kitty." Basically, they'd be back to working for their mom for room, board, and love.

"I'll see what I can borrow." Carson let his booted foot slide off his knee and thump on the floor. "If we can pay the debts back quickly, the interest won't be the end of the world. Especially if it saves the ranch."

"So," Jill slapped her hands on her jeans, "if you guys are all agreed this is the best plan, I'll be a team player, go along, but I want it on the record that if this blows up in our faces, I thought before, and still think, it's a crazy idea."

"Noted." Carson smiled at his sister.

"Who's going to break the news to Garret and Kade?" Rachel raised one brow at her siblings.

Preston exhaled. "If Sarah and I are going through with this, telling Garret can wait till his vacation is over. Poor guy spends most of the year dealing with classrooms of junior high tweens, he deserves time. Kade can wait till we figure out all the details."

Jill spun around to face Sarah. Concern warred with intense determination. Determination was winning. "You do realize what you're volunteering for?"

"To help save the ranch."

He wished Sarah had sounded a little more sure of her answer.

Jill crossed her arms and shook her head once from left to right. "To play footsies with my brother."

The words "It's not like that," spilled from Preston's mouth at the same time Sarah Sue protested, "It wouldn't be like that."

Jill held up her hand. "Maybe not when you're home, but if you're going to convince the bank, the town, *and* Mom that you're enough in love to want to marry and marry fast, you're going to have to play the part in public—a lot."

This plan was not the same as being a fill-in for one night. This would be an entire year—after they married. "She's right." Preston shrugged.

Sarah Sue seemed to be making an effort just to nod.

He didn't like that. "We should probably talk."

She nodded again.

Rachel pushed to her feet. "And I should check on Mom."

"Yes," Jill followed her sister, "she may be feeling hungry. With all the commotion, we sort of forgot about dinner."

"I'll help you." Carson hurried after Jill, leaving Preston and Sarah Sue alone.

He considered whether or not he should remain across the room or move closer, unsure if that would make the talk they needed to have easier or more difficult. The internal debate almost made him laugh. How was he supposed to play house with a woman who he was afraid to sit next to? "Are you hungry?"

Pretty blue eyes widened with surprise, blinked, and one side of her mouth tipped upward in a half-hearted smile. "Actually, I am."

"Good. Grab your purse. We'll talk in the car on the way to the café. That should give you twenty minutes to decide whether or not you want to go through with this hare-brained idea."

CHAPTER SIX

Out the door and climbing into the front seat of Preston's car, since she and Preston had never actually dated—not even close—any moment Sarah expected a wave of awkward discomfort to settle in. They were four years apart and he treated her the same way he had his kid sisters. The day before senior prom her date had broken his ankle. She'd been so upset at the idea of going without a date that Ms. Alice had turned to Preston, who, of course, had stepped in to save the day. He'd been a good sport about it and had gone the whole nine yards to make the night special. And proved to be a much better dancer than her at the time boyfriend. For months afterward a handful of townsfolk who'd seen them together had made it a point to let her know she shouldn't have let him get away. As if she'd ever had him.

Those same gossips were fueled when the year before she'd moved to Austin, he'd needed a last-minute date for a couples event at his then-new job. After all, one good turn deserved another, and she volunteered. Considering how often he'd saved her, it seemed only fair she should do the same at least once, though the truth was, she was more than happy to spend some one-on-one time with Preston. They'd had a great time catching up and she'd had the best time since her prom. Nice guys were hard to find and he was genuinely a nice guy. Considering his willingness to marry anyone to save the family ranch, he'd remained a nice guy.

The passenger door slammed shut and a knot formed in her stomach. Preston circled the hood and settled in the driver's seat. Her palms grew moist. Even though Alice Sweet had stepped in as absentee mother after the accident that took the life of Sarah's mother, maybe marrying the woman's son to save the ranch that meant so much to all of them wasn't the brightest idea she'd ever had. Not that giving up a year of her life would matter much. Her last date had been over six months ago and nothing worth repeating. Wiping her hands down the side of her jeans, she dared to look over at Preston. Hand on the steering wheel, he wasn't quite smiling, but he appeared way more calm than she felt. Like he was thinking about some long-ago pleasant memory. A time when life was good, easier, maybe even happier. Then again, for all she knew about him, he could have been thinking about the final score of last night's ball game.

Either way, he turned the ignition key and twisted to face her. Deep blue eyes settled on hers, and he seemed to quietly promise everything would be fine. Like he'd done so many years ago, he'd take care of her. The tangled knot in her stomach quickly unraveled. Any anxious thoughts faded away.

"I admit, I'm not sure where to start." He chuckled softly. "Not every day I have to hash out a temporary life on the short drive to town."

"Temporary life," she repeated. "I suppose that's as good a definition as any."

He reached over and threaded his fingers with hers, settling their joined hands on the console. "We're going to have to do this a lot if we go through with the plan."

Staring down at their laced fingers, she nodded, a little surprised at how comfortable, almost normal, the small gesture felt.

"Whenever we're in public I'll be expected to hold your hand, occasionally put an arm around you."

She nodded. When she realized he was continuously glancing in her direction to read her reactions, she blew out a soft sigh and found her words. "I understand. We're playing a part. Like a very long-running play."

"Yes." He nodded. "I suppose that's exactly what it's like. But, we don't have to decide everything on this ride, or even tonight, but we should get a few generalities out of the way to help you make up your mind."

She'd already made up her mind. Though some might feel it was too late to make any decisions as she'd already lost whatever little bit of mind she might have had left.

The next few miles were driven in silence. She imagined they were each scanning their thoughts for potential problems and pitfalls, though she couldn't really come up with anything. Instead she shifted her thoughts to logistics. "Where will we live?"

Eyes wide, he blinked and then blew out a deep breath. "It had been my intention to move into the ranch house to help with the early morning work load. But under the new circumstances, even if the commute is going to be a bear, my apartment makes the most sense. Though, fair warning, I haven't ever really gotten around to…um, decorating. The place still has the furniture from my college apartment, but it's our best option."

Understanding that meant waking up in what would most likely be the middle of the night in order to be at the ranch before the crack of dawn, she reluctantly nodded. It would be for the better. "At least there won't be anyone living with us, watching every move we make."

"What about your place in Austin?"

So caught up in the good deed of a lifetime, she had forgotten about her cute little apartment in Barton Hills, or that her approval to work from her family home could be yanked at any time. "If it will make things look more legit, I could cancel my lease and look for something new when this is all over."

"Then you're not home permanently?"

She shrugged. "At the moment, I'm for sure here for at least the next few months, but during the pandemic, work from home didn't have a major impact so we've been told that barring something unexpected, there are no plans to require us to work from the main office if we don't have to. I'm hoping to be able to move back for good though. Austin was fun at first, but, even without the ruby slippers, there's no place like home."

One corner of his mouth held a shaky smile. "I see."

"Do you think the uncertainty is a problem?"

Those lips she'd spent way more time than she should have staring at, flattened into a thin line for a long moment before he shook his head. "Honestly, in this world of telecommuting and short-haul commutes, I can't think of any reason this would be a major obstacle. In real life things happen; when it happens, we'll deal with it."

"Excellent point." Already Sarah liked the way they were able to work things out. So far the sort-of-almost marriage was looking good.

"If we go through with this," he cast a side glance in her direction again, "the fewer people who know the better. Less chance for a slip of the tongue."

"Agreed."

He squeezed her hand for a split second, sending electric shocks up her arm and at the same time, a comforting warmth to soothe her. "What about your dad? Could you handle not telling him?"

And wasn't that an excellent question. For the most part, she didn't keep any secrets from her father. Then again, sharing details of her love life—not that this arrangement could be considered a love life—but if she had one, sharing wasn't something she did with her dad. In that sense keeping the arrangement to herself was easy. On the other hand, it could break her father's heart to not be included until the day they filed for divorce. *Divorce.* She would be a divorced woman after this. Not that it mattered in this day and age, but she didn't like failure and somehow the word divorce and failure were synonymous in her mind. Yet, how could she fail at a fake marriage? An annulment would be better, but then would they have to give the money back? Lord, her mind was out of breath batting all the thoughts back and forth.

"You okay? Change your mind yet?"

She had no idea if he was worried or hopeful. His tone gave away nothing. "Just more questions, but I don't think I'd be comfortable keeping something this important from my dad."

Lips pressed tightly together, eyes back on the road, he nodded.

Suddenly, she was the one worried he'd change his mind. "Dad's a doctor. He's maintained doctor patient confidences for decades. I'm sure he could keep our secret."

The tension in Preston's jaw eased and slowly, he bobbed his head again. "I'm sure you're right. Your father isn't exactly the town gossip."

That made Sarah chuckle. Iris Hathaway came to mind. Tall, lean yet curvaceous, with big blonde Texas hair and an accent that gave away her Georgia roots, the woman could spread any news faster than the Associated Press. She and Sarah's father most definitely had nothing in common. "Then we're in agreement to tell my father?"

Preston nodded. "And you still haven't changed your mind?"

She shook her head. It felt good to make progress. Two big issues were settled and put aside. Accomplishing that much would have made her smile, except for the million other smaller things they still had to figure out—and sooner was definitely better.

Having pulled into the parking lot beside the café, Preston turned into the nearest space and undid his safety belt. Not till he felt the empty caress of cool air against his skin did he realize Sarah Sue had pulled her hand out of his to release her own seatbelt.

To avoid reaching for her again, he shoved both hands in his pants pockets. At some point they were going to need to get started showing themselves around town as a couple, but not till they were one hundred percent on board with no cause to back out. For whatever reason, he felt like an awkward teen on a first date. It made no sense, but he needed to shake it off and move forward. Grabbing the front door, he waved Sarah Sue inside.

Even on a weekday evening, the café did a brisk business. Before Agnes, the waitress who had been serving the town for as long as Preston could remember, could motion for them to pick any table, half a dozen people had waved, nodded, or grinned at him.

Mildred McEntire had come running up to Sarah Sue and pulled her into a tight hug. The woman wore so much bling, she could have illuminated the way for a lost ship on a fog-heavy night. "Aren't you looking pretty as a picture?" The grinning woman beamed at Sarah Sue.

Strangers watching might have thought the two hadn't seen each other in decades rather than during Sarah Sue's last visit home.

His pretty neighbor's cheeks pinkened at the compliment as she waved an arm at Mildred. "I love the outfit."

Turning left then right so the light from above reflected off every shimmering trinket, Mildred grinned from ear to ear. "Made it myself."

"Very nice," Sarah Sue confirmed with a smile.

Mildred's gaze shifted, she gave a fast smile in Preston's direction that teetered on a knowing smirk before scurrying back to the table of friends, including Iris Hathaway, now waving frantically at her to hurry up.

"Well." Sarah Sue blew out a slow sigh. "By the end of the day, I'm betting Mildred will have seen to it personally that the whole town knows we were in here together and Iris will have at least half of them convinced we're not only matrimony-bound but will be raising twins by morning."

"For probably the first time in my life," he held back a chuckle, "I hope you're right."

Resisting the instinct to place his hand on the small of her back, for now, Preston pointed to a booth in the far corner of the café. The spot offered some semblance of privacy. Which he knew most likely would feed the gossip mill.

"I don't know why I'm looking at this menu." Sarah Sue perused every item with the same intensity as if studying for a final exam. "I know everything on it. The café hasn't changed the menu since I was a little kid."

"I'm not sure she changed it before that." Preston chuckled, his smile fading and spine stiffening at the sharp whistle-like siren that sounded through town. He glanced at his phone to see if he was being called in. Nothing. "Probably another false alarm."

"Another?"

"Last time the fire alarm sounded, it was the middle of the night. Pretty much the entire volunteer fire department answered the call, me included, only to arrive at Mrs. Carmichael's house and discover it wasn't on fire at all. She'd called because her cat had somehow gotten into the attic crawl space and was trapped in the rafters and she was worried."

"Cats get trapped in rafters? I've never known a cat that couldn't maneuver in the darnedest, and highest, of places, and then eventually land on their feet."

"Considering the cat darted past the crew the moment the firemen opened the crawl space door, I would say you still haven't known of a cat that couldn't find her way out of an attic crawl space the same way she got in."

The only full-time fire department personnel was the chief, and when his SUV flew down Main Street with the lights flashing and the siren blaring, chairs scraped the floor as people pushed away from the tables and hurried to the café windows. Whatever was on fire—if it was on fire—the structure was in town.

"That doesn't sound like it's another cat," Sarah Sue said softly.

The hairs on the back of his neck stood at full attention. The same way his gut had churned earlier in the day with concern for his mom, a bristly feeling told him there was more trouble on the horizon.

Lips pressed tightly together, Sarah Sue shook her head. "This could become a big deal fast. Some of the older buildings in town are so ancient, they'd light up like kindling doused with gasoline."

Eyes narrowed, Preston focused his gaze out the windows in the direction the fire chief had gone. He didn't want to tell her that he'd thought the same thing, and wondered if the paging system was down since only the town alarm sounded to summon the volunteers. By the time a thin layer of smoke began to drift across town in their direction, he knew his gut had been right for the second time today.

He was already sliding out of the booth and on his feet when one of the town's two fire trucks raced past the diner with the second truck not far behind. "I'd better see if they need help."

Sarah nodded and followed him out of the booth. "I haven't been through training like you and the other volunteer firemen, but even if all I can offer up is moral support, I'll be first in line."

For a fraction of a moment he considered how to tell her to stay put, she'd only be in the way, and then he just as quickly remembered who he was talking about. Sarah Sue Conroy was one of the most competent people he knew. She might not know much about fighting fires, but with her father out delivering a baby, she'd know more about doctoring anyone injured than most folks. He extended his hand. "Come on. We'll go out the back, take the alley, avoid the lookie-loos."

They'd barely made it out the door when Preston realized the plume of smoke originated from across the street and up the road a piece. The same direction as his apartment. He picked up the pace, rushing at a near trot, oblivious to almost dragging Sarah Sue behind him until he got to his block, saw the black smoke and orange flames spewing from the broken glass windows of his apartment, and heard Sarah Sue's ragged breaths, followed by a loud gasp.

Neighbors near and far gathered on the corner. Because it was his apartment, the fire chief wouldn't let him participate in the efforts. Gripping Sarah Sue's hand tighter than he probably should have, he was surprised to find he was glad to have her here, and that he didn't want to let go.

Leaning against him, her other hand crossed in front of her and rested on his upper arm. The slow movement of her fingers swirled a soothing sensation that stayed the sense of loss building inside him. First the dread from his mother's fall, then the heartbreak at the threat of losing a ranch that had been in the family for centuries, and now, as meagerly decorated at is it was, what had been his home for the last several years was literally crumbling before him. At least most of the prized possessions from his youth were still at the ranch.

Her head now resting on his shoulder, she squeezed his hand. The gesture saying so much more than words could.

"So sorry, Preston." One of the members of the ladies auxiliary glanced from the charred building and the smoking embers to Preston, then not as casually as she may have wanted, her gaze dropped to their tightly woven hands, up to Sarah Sue's head still resting against his shoulder and back to Preston. "I know you've got lots of support," her glance darted briefly again to Sarah Sue who had straightened at his side, but still held on to his hand, "but if you need anything at all. Anything. You can count on all of us."

Preston nodded, the reality of the situation handing him another blow. With apartments so hard to come by in this community and no place to live anymore outside of the scrutiny of others, this not so little fire no doubt just put the kibosh on their plans for a pretend marriage. And wasn't that just a damn shame.

"There you two are." Iris Hathaway came rushing up to him, Mildred on her heels. "I couldn't have been more flustered to hear of all people, your home was the one to have set off the alarm. And you were having such a nice date too."

His jaw dropped, ready to inform the unofficial town crier that they were not a couple, when Sarah Sue spoke up. Chin high and a sweet smile on her face, his almost fake bride leveled her eyes with his, and not looking back at Iris, clearly uttered, "Yes, we were."

Not the words he'd expected, he was even more surprised under the circumstances when the two women smiled.

"Well, it's about time you two got together. I always said you made the cutest prom couple ever." Iris muttered a polite *have to run* and scurried off no doubt ready to announce to the world. Apparently, apartment be danged. Whatever details they might need to newly hash out, none of it seemed to matter. Sarah Sue had just done the Honeysuckle Texas version of announcing to the world they were an item.

CHAPTER SEVEN

"**M**om, you should not be up. Especially not cooking."

Alice Sweet waved a hand at her son. "What kind of mother would I be if I stayed in bed and let you fend for yourself on today of all days?"

"Today is no different than any other day." Stepping around Brady perched comfortably at her feet, Preston sidled up beside his mom and carefully touching her arm, tried to ease the spatula out of her hand.

"No you don't. Though the circumstances aren't the best, I'm glad to have you back at the ranch. A little help in your spare time will be nice, but right now, your heart may be in the right place, but face it dear, you cook up better spreadsheets than pancakes."

On both counts, his mom was spot on. Even though he knew his way around the kitchen well enough not to starve, he wasn't going to win a home-cooking contest anytime soon, though living at the ranch would make helping easier. With so many people displaced from one of the few apartment buildings in town, there was little hope of finding anywhere else to stay. In terms of helping out his mother, that was great. As for his and Sarah Sue's little charade, this brought a whole new dilemma to the plans. Still, that didn't need to be solved right now and his mother overdoing it did. "I'd really feel better if you went back to bed and let me—"

"Oh, I'm late." Sarah Sue came in the back door with a large foil-covered tray in her hand. "I knew you had a house to feed this morning so I made extra sausage and hash browns."

"That's sweet of you. I appreciate the thoughtfulness,

but I'm feeling much better today."

Preston let his gaze meet Sarah Sue's. He was pretty sure the doctor's orders had not been *feel free to go back to running a ranch in the morning.* When Sarah gave the slightest shake of her head, he knew his mom was not being a good patient.

"Why does what's cooking smell so good?" Rachel came bounding down the stairs. "Mom, you are not supposed to be up. Doc said you should take it easy for a few days."

"I am. There's nothing hard about flipping pancakes."

His sister's gaze met his. If she wanted answers from him on how to get their mother to hand over the spatula and go back to bed, his sister was plum out of luck.

"Ms. Alice, if I go home and my father finds out I let you cook breakfast, I may find my bags packed and set on the front porch." Sarah set the foil-covered pan on the counter and leaned over to scratch the scruff of Brady's neck.

His mom blinked. And she might even have winced when she turned at the waist without moving her feet.

"She's right, Mom. Doc is always grumbling about patients who don't take his advice." Rachel came forward and gently reached for the spatula.

"It's not like I had open heart surgery." His mom tightened her grip on the spatula and flipped a row of pancakes before looking at her daughter. "If you want to help, you can save me a few steps and start cracking eggs."

"I'll set the table." Preston turned toward the cupboard.

By the time Carson and Jillian had joined them in the kitchen and the pancakes were warming in the oven, they'd managed to convince their mother to at least sit while they finished cooking breakfast.

Sarah Sue had glanced more than once at Preston and smiled. Coincidentally at just the moment when his mom had been looking up. "I'd better get back home and let Dad know everything here is under control."

"Of course it is." His mom smiled. "Tell your dad I said thanks, and I'm fine."

The door had hardly latched shut behind Sarah Sue when his mother shifted her attention to Preston. "Best neighbors a family could ever ask for."

No one in the room could deny that.

"Mildred tells me you two were having dinner at the café."

He knew Mildred worked fast, but it was only six o'clock in the morning and his mother had been sleeping soundly last night, both when he and Sarah Sue left and when he'd finally come home in the middle of the night.

"When did Mildred find the time to report my dinner plans with you?"

Reaching for a pancake, his mom shrugged. "Makes no never mind. You two seem to be rather cozy this morning."

This would be the time when normally he or any of his siblings would redirect their mom, but he had to remind himself that there was a plan that needed to be put in place and this was exactly what they'd all hoped for. For a split second he hated deceiving his mother, but this was one of those altruistic moments about the greater good. "She followed the alarm with me. With doc delivering a baby across town, we thought she might be of help."

His mom lifted one brow. It was the same look she'd give him when he was a kid making excuses for showing up late for supper, chores, or anything else that involved a little fast—or not so fast—thinking on his feet. He wasn't sure how she did it, but even though he was a full-grown adult, that look still made him as nervous as a kid caught with his hand in the cookie jar.

"That's why she was with me when I learned the apartment was on fire."

Her brow still arched high, his mom's chin dipped, her gaze remained fixed with his and he swallowed hard. He could do this. Take it slow, play the part. "She's a good friend."

"Is everything a total loss?" Doing what the siblings normally did to help redirect their parents away from a brother or sister on the hot seat, Jillian stabbed at some eggs on her plate.

"No idea. Things have to cool down, then the engineers have to determine if it's safe to even go near the building, never mind rummage through my apartment. But I'm doubtful whatever survived the fire will have survived the water soaking."

Jillian sighed. "I'm really sorry about the fire, but look on the bright side, moving back here, you won't have to pay rent."

That seemed to make his mother come the closest to smiling she'd done all morning. "Good thing so many of your things are still here. Otherwise you'd be borrowing your brothers' clothes this morning."

Her attention successfully diverted to a safer—for now—topic, his mom gingerly cut at the edge of her pancake. He'd noticed she'd even been chewing slowly. Between the deliberate movements and lack of appetite, he had little doubt that his mom was hurting more than she was letting on.

All the kids had moved out, though none had had the heart to fully empty their rooms. Preston was no exception, and yet, he never thought there would come a day when whatever was left in his old room would be pretty much all he had. Hopefully, the next part of the plan would easily unfold his mother's natural suspicions. However things progressed, they'd better do so quickly because with every tick of the clock, this family was running out of time.

"Are you ready?" Standing at the passenger door, Preston held his hand out for Sarah Sue.

She'd been settling into her new role all day. Well, technically, most of the night too as visions of a pretend life with Preston filled both her waking thoughts and what little sleeping moments she'd had. The silent communication first thing this morning had taken her by surprise at first, but by the time she'd returned home, she'd reminded herself that of all the brothers, she'd always somehow felt more connected to Preston. Then she'd spent the rest of her day casually bringing Preston's name up with every conversation she'd had, even folks who didn't live in town or have a clue who he was. What she hadn't worked out was when to sit down with her father. Sooner than later would probably be best, but for now, the second night of the big charade was on. "As ready as I'll ever be."

Her hand slid easily into his and without hesitation, their fingers intertwined. Somehow this felt more natural to Sarah than walking on her own, hands free.

Tonight, rather than the café, they'd chosen the Main Street Steakhouse for dinner. Though it was unlikely they'd run into Mildred or Iris here on a weeknight, there was no doubt their evening out would find its way onto the grapevine just as quickly nonetheless.

Preston leaned in as they reached the door. "I thought I'd ask for a booth. Implies a need for privacy."

"Sit next to me too."

His eyes widened a moment before his head tipped with questions.

"Friends sit across from each other, married people sit across from each other, but—"

"People dating sit side by side," Preston finished her thought and nodded briefly. "Side by side it is."

What she hadn't given any thought to was how hard it might be sitting so close to Preston that she could feel the warmth of his thigh spreading through her slacks and inching its way through her system all the way to her fingertips and toes.

"How'd your day go?" Preston smiled at her before reaching for the menu.

"Fine except for a troubled K-9. I'm running out of options for him."

"K-9?" It took a second for Preston to mull over her words. "That's right. You work with a non-profit, don't you?"

"I do. And I'm tasked with rehoming and retraining troubled service dogs to be able to be adopted by ordinary families, but it's not easy finding interim places for them."

"Admirable." After a quick perusal, he set the menu on the table. "Brady had a hard time adjusting to ranch life after his stint as a military dog."

"I know it put Kade at ease having your family take care of Brady. Your mom did a great job with him."

"That she did. Mom is amazing." His expression slipped. "I can't imagine what we'd have done if yesterday had turned out differently, if we hadn't found her so soon."

"Well, don't think about that. Your mom is tough and that attitude will help speed her recovery. I just wish it were in time for Samson."

"Samson?"

"The latest K-9 with PTSD issues. I have to go check him out tomorrow. I was hoping I could get your mom to take him on, but I can't ask in her condition."

"Why not?"

"German Shepherds with PTSD can be a handful, and Samson is a big boy. Your mom would need all her strength to work with him."

"What about me? I can help. So can my siblings."

"Don't you think y'all have your hands full enough at the moment?"

"We do, but I know from Kade and Brady that service dogs deserve as much of our respect and gratitude as the men in combat boots. If you don't find someone, what will happen to him?"

That she didn't want to think about. "As a very last resort, he could be put down to make way for other dogs coming into the program with better odds of rehabilitation. At the moment there's a Tuesday deadline."

"Then I guess it's settled. If Mom agrees, we're all in. Can I come with you tomorrow?"

This time she tipped her head in thought. "It's not the usual procedure. The groups that take the dogs that failed original transition programs frown on too much interaction from strangers that could set the dogs off and put visitors in peril." She wasn't going to say or setback whatever progress might have been made with the dogs.

"Makes sense," he said. "But can I come?"

That made her chuckle. "Determined, aren't you?"

Preston shrugged. "I am my mama's boy."

"Okay. Tomorrow you can tag along, but don't be surprised if you're not let out of the car."

"Fair enough."

Over dinner, enough people stopped at the table to give Preston their condolences for the fire as well as giving well wishes for his mother's quick recovery. A few people probably volunteered more than they should have, expressing how much misfortune could one family take. First his dad, then his mom's injuries, and now the fire, but compared to the stinging loss of his dad, losing his bachelor possessions was nothing. Preston dutifully thanked each and everyone for their concern. Every so often, he'd squeeze his and Sarah's joined hands for all to see. Well, everyone could see they were holding hands, but it was unlikely they knew when he squeezed her hand, which had her wondering was that extra gesture for show or for real.

"Where to now?" Preston slipped money into the check on the table and slid out of the booth.

"Not home?"

Extending his hand to her, he shook his head, and pulled her in close, whispering into her ear, "We have a town to convince."

"Walk in the park." Not much else could be done in this small town at this hour.

A smile took over his face. "Great idea." Taking a short stroll down Main Street, Preston took in the familiar surroundings. They passed his sister's store. She'd been so excited when the space opened up and she was able to begin her dream of being her own boss. Just past the candle shop was his aunts' place. He had no idea how Honeysuckle had become the state capital for the game, but ever since he was a kid anything corn hole had been a very big deal, so, of course, his aunts Liz and Vicki's business had been an anchor on Main Street. He also remembered as a kid the town's huge fight over whether or not to pave over the old cobblestone sidewalks. At the time he could not have cared less what they decided, but now, walking down the old bricked sidewalk, he was glad the preservation side had won. Reaching the park, he knew just what to do next and tugged her over to the corn hole courts.

Staring at the area, she wondered if he was teasing her. "Wouldn't you rather sit on a bench or something?"

He shook his head and grinned like the Cheshire Cat. "Nope. Let's see what you've got."

"Oh, really." Her hesitation slipped away at the veiled challenge. She wouldn't have the job she did if she didn't like a challenge. "You're on."

Manipulating the weighted bags, Preston handed her the dark green set. "To match your eyes."

Had that come from anyone else, any other time, she'd have been appropriately intrigued, even flattered, but under the odd circumstances, she had no idea what to make of the fact that at some point, he'd noticed she had green eyes. "Then blue for you."

His head bobbed as he waved for her to take the first turn.

It had been years since she'd played, but if all went well, tossing would be akin to riding a bike—you never forget. Her first shot slid off the board and over the edge. Maybe riding a bike was easier.

Preston chuckled and took his shot. Though it didn't slide off the board, the bag didn't land in a hole either. With a bashful grin, he shrugged one shoulder at her.

Two more turns came and went, and with each one, they giggled just a little harder. When Preston began horsing around, and standing sideways, would toss the bags from behind his back, the bags landed every which way, occasionally on the board. The shenanigans had the two of them almost doubled over with laughter.

"Were you always this ridiculous?" She could not stop laughing.

"You mean skilled?"

"Considering I haven't played in years and am whooping your behind, I'm not sure skilled is the right word for your performance."

Straightening to his full height, Preston lifted one of the

bags from a nearby table carved from an old tree stump. Tossing it lightly in the air, testing the feel of it, he turned to the boards and eyeing the distance carefully, lobbed the bag. A hole in one. Then slowly, he turned again, facing her, a cocky grin taking over his face.

"You've been holding out on me." She marched up to him and shaking her head, planted her fists on her hips. "You *let* me win."

Failing miserably at biting back a smile, he shrugged. "You know what they say, happy wife, happy life."

Rolling her eyes, she blew out a sigh. "Not yet."

He stepped in closer to her. "Let me show you why you're overshooting." Another bean bag in hand, he repositioned himself behind her, and in a quick solitary move, dropped the bag into her hand while taking hold of her wrist.

She wasn't sure what had her more startled, the feel of his body up close and very personally against hers, or the warmth of his breath fanning her neck.

"Think of it like bowling. Keep your thumb forward." Still holding on to her, he swung her arm gently forward then back. "Put too much force into it and you'll blow over your target."

"Target," she managed to mumble despite her heightened senses.

One more time, he moved her arm forward then back. "That's right. Now, on the forward motion, open your fingers and let the bag slide out of your hand." Still holding on to her, he guided her movement, only letting go of her hand as it swung forward, seconds before releasing the bag. Not a hole in one, but the bag slid alongside and teetering on the edge, slowly tipped into the hole.

"You mean like that?" Twisting about, her face turned and she found herself only inches away from those mesmerizing blue eyes. She stood frozen in place. Unable to move, or think, or speak.

The sudden flash of light in his gaze told her that he'd been caught as much off guard by their proximity as she had. Staring into her eyes, he gazed long and hard before blinking, clearing his throat, and taking a step in retreat. "Yeah, like that."

Her gaze followed him to the basket of bags and for the first time since they came up with this save the ranch plan, Sarah wondered if maybe she was seriously in over her head.

CHAPTER EIGHT

Rolling his head left then right, Preston blew out a long, slow breath. Nothing in his memories of working the ranch at his father's side included so many sore muscles. He had just enough time to drink a strong cup of coffee, shower, and change before meeting Sarah for the trip to see the troubled dog. A couple of aspirin was also probably a good idea. Lingering in the hot shower a little longer than usual might not be a horrible prospect either.

"You look like you've seen better days." His mom sat at the table with a cup of coffee cradled in her hands.

"You're supposed to be resting." Preston poured himself a cup and eased into a seat near his mother.

"If I rest anymore, I'll turn into an overstuffed pillow. This is fine. I'm fine."

"Mom—"

Alice Sweet's hand shot up, palm out, cutting her son off. "Yes, I'm still sore. Yes, I need time to fully heal, but I am most definitely fine. A few cuts and bruises aren't going to kill me."

A small part of him had to agree with her assessment, but another part of him knew that an injured body needed both time and rest to heal. "Couldn't you at least take it easy on the sofa?"

"It doesn't hurt as much if I move around. When I stay still and then move, I remember why I hurt."

"Which is why you should go back to bed."

His mom rolled her eyes and took a slow sip of her coffee. He suspected more from discomfort than savoring the brew. "Sarah Sue called."

"She did?" He hoped that sounded casually guarded.

"She knew y'all were out working the cattle, so she called the landline. Something came up with work so she's running a little behind. She'll pick you up in about an hour."

Unsure of what to say, he gave a quick nod.

A small smile teased one corner of his mother's mouth. "I heard you were at the park last night."

He bobbed his head again.

"You like her."

It wasn't a question but he nodded again nonetheless. That much wasn't a lie or subterfuge. He really did like Sarah Sue. Always had, but maybe now a little more than he'd realized.

"Where are you going today?"

"To evaluate a dog. A military dog who needs to be rehomed but he has issues that basically equate to PTSD in a human."

"And what are you going to do?"

He shrugged. "Watch?"

That smile tugged at her lips again. "I see." Just as the smile had appeared, it quickly slipped away. "I've been thinking a bit, you know, about the ranch situation, and playing with numbers. I want to run some ideas by you and the others. Maybe after dinner?"

How he wished he could tell her that they already had a plan in the works, but a simple nod was all he could offer.

Her smile reappeared. "Good. Then go."

From the twinkle in her eye and the stubborn streak he was too familiar with, he knew she was working on a plan of her own. "You're not going to lie down, are you?"

She shook her head.

All he could do was sigh. Hopefully, his mother would heal up faster than anyone expected, because debating her care with her was not going well for either of them. As much as he hated leaving his mother alone, she was right, he had a date with a hot shower. Pushing to his feet, he leaned over and gently kissed her cheek. "I love you."

Her smile bloomed. "Love you more."

Despite his desire to melt under the hot shower, Preston

needed to be dressed and downstairs before Sarah arrived. Seated on the edge of his bed, he slipped on one boot then the other and stood. Taking a moment to glance in the mirror, he double-checked that his shirt tail wasn't out or his fly down. Convinced he was ready to go, he reached for the doorknob and could hear Sarah talking to his mother in the kitchen.

"Poor baby," his mother cooed.

"It's hard enough for some of these dogs to go from working dogs to family pets, but toss in emotional issues or just plain fearfulness, and the transition is even more challenging." Sarah stood facing his mother, her back against the counter. "I wish we had a facility like the one near Dallas, but even they can't save every dog."

His mother shifted in her seat, did a poor job of hiding a pained wince. "Maybe that's something we should work toward."

"There are so many military working dogs as well as contract working dogs or police dogs." Sarah sighed. "So many."

"Maybe, once we get through a few projects and hire a new foreman, I can help."

From where Preston stopped at the kitchen entry, he could see the sweet smile bloom on Sarah's face in response to his mother's reply, igniting a smile of his own, and a few other things. Agreement or no agreement, he was going to have to be very careful to watch his Ps and Qs or this whole marriage bargain could blow up in everyone's face.

At the sound of Preston's throat clearing from the doorway, Sarah glanced up at him and the sweetest smile took over her face. Boy, was she good at this game.

"Hi." Preston debated walking over to her, but instead shifted his attention from her to his mother as he leaned over and kissed his mom on the cheek. "We have a long drive ahead of us, so we'll be heading out."

"Of course." His mother smiled at him, her gaze darted to Sarah Sue and the smile brightened just a little. How he wished he didn't have to deceive his mother, but it was for the good of the ranch she and his dad, like all the generations before them, loved so dearly.

He debated extending his arm to Sarah, but had a different idea instead. Turning on his heel as Sarah said her goodbyes to his mother, they walked out the back door toward his parked car. When he'd come to the edge of the porch, he stopped and snatched Sarah's hand, turning her to face him. "Mom can still see us from her seat and I'm betting she's watching. Knowing her stubborn streak, she might even have stood up to get closer to the window, so forgive me." Without another word, he pulled her snuggly against him and gave her a tender kiss on the lips, just long enough to make his mother happy without being too much for a first kiss. Slowly, he eased back and not saying a word, gave her hand a slight tug and walked them to the car.

Not till they were off the ranch land and on the main road did he turn to her. "Are you okay?"

She nodded.

"Was that too much?"

Still silent, her gaze ahead, Sarah shook her head.

"Do you want to change your mind?"

Her head whipped around to face him, her eyes filled with questions he couldn't begin to decipher.

"We don't have to go through with this, but if we do, we're going to be living at the ranch and putting on a show like that until I can secure living arrangements elsewhere. And with everyone in my building looking for a new place to crash, that won't be easy."

She blew out a slow sigh. "No, it won't."

"So where do we go from here?"

Somehow Sarah Sue doubted running off to Vegas and staying there was the answer he wanted. Well, maybe the Vegas part would be fine, but not returning until the year was over and the trust money was in the bank was not an option. "I'll plug the coordinates for the transition shelter into my phone."

His shoulders tensed and she knew she shouldn't have been so casual.

"Sorry."

He shook his head, but didn't speak.

"I'll get used to all of this. It will be fine. We can do this." Lord, at least she hoped she could. When she first spotted him standing at the entrance to the kitchen, all she could think was damn that man knew how to fill a doorway.

This time, Preston pressed his lips tightly together and nodded his head. A few more minutes of total silence and he cleared his throat again. "I don't want anything to hurt our friendship. Anything."

On that they could agree. "Ditto."

"This may be harder than I first thought."

What? Kissing her, being affectionate, lying to his mother, working the ranch and his day job, the dog?

His gaze shifted to hers and his shoulders deflated. "I'm sorry. I'm just realizing the enormity of what we've gotten ourselves into."

Wasn't that the truth? Suddenly hiding the charade from their parents seemed like the least of their challenges. "Do you want to back out?"

Without a moment's hesitation, he shook his head. "This is our best chance of saving the ranch."

"Then save the ranch we shall. Maybe we can save Samson too."

The rest of the drive was filled with mundane chatter intertwined with memories and twenty questions. By the time they reached the shelter, they knew each other's favorite colors, favorite foods, favorite movies, most pleasant memories and most embarrassing memories. They discovered they both adored having Mr. Wheeler for history and could have done with anyone but Mrs. Mahoney for biology.

"I'll never forget the day I walked into her office to buy the tickets for the school play." Preston chuckled. "I was a freshman and had no clue who this woman was, other than one of the biology teachers. I did as I had been taught, smiled charmingly at her and asked for two tickets. When she stared at me a moment and then said, "You're a freshman, aren't you?" I wondered if she was psychic or if someone had pinned a *kick me I'm a freshman* note somewhere that I hadn't noticed."

"Did you? Have a note on you?"

He shook his head. "Nope. I asked her, 'Do I look that clueless?' Then she frowned and replied, 'No, you're smiling at me.'"

Sarah couldn't hold back the burst of laughter that erupted. "Oh, I can so picture Mrs. Mahoney saying that. She really did have a mean streak."

"I considered that perhaps it was just my perspective as a student and I'd understand better once I grew up."

"Did you?"

"Nope. After a decade I concluded she was just plain mean."

"Honestly, your charming smile can be quite persuasive. If that didn't win her over, nothing would."

"Thank you." He reached over and touched her hand. "We're going to be okay, aren't we?"

She grinned. "I really do think so."

The rescue organization allowed Preston to sit on a bench outside a chain link fenced area to watch Sarah Sue's interactions with the dog in question. From what he could see, the animal was a stunning specimen of a German Shepherd. Thick neck, mixed coat, and dark face that would have scared the bejesus out of any ferocious creature.

In complete contrast the dog was stiff, unresponsive, almost trying to hide in the dirt beneath his feet. The temperament looked nothing like what Preston expected from a military dog. The man holding the leash, Aaron, had to practically drag the canine to meet Sarah. Finally, the man sat on the ground, made a tsking noise to call the dog, and head down, not making eye contact, slowly the animal crept toward the trainer. When Samson was close enough for the man to touch, he scratched at the dog's scruff and though still clearly apprehensive, the dog seemed to relax at least a little.

Sarah immediately squatted where she stood, her gaze riveted on the animal. Finally, pushing to her feet, she called out to the man, "Where do you kennel him?"

Leaving the dog where he laid, Aaron walked up to where Sarah stood, still watching the animal. "He has his own area."

"So this is not familiar to him?"

Aaron shook his head.

"Can I see him in a familiar to him setting?"

Hefting one shoulder the trainer shrugged, then cast his gaze in Preston's direction. "Just one of you?"

Sarah glanced over her shoulder at Preston and he could tell she was debating her next move. When her shoulders relaxed and she momentarily blinked her eyes shut, he knew exactly what she'd been thinking: if he was to help retrain this dog, how the dog interacted with Preston was potentially more important than how he reacted to Sarah. Her head bobbed. "Both of us is best."

Aaron hesitated so long that Preston thought he might say no. Finally, he looked to Sarah. "If you're sure."

As Preston crossed the yard toward Sarah, he got a better look at the dog. Once he stopped by Sarah's side, he smiled. "I thought Brady was a handsome boy, but this fellow is gorgeous."

"Brady?" the man asked.

"My brother's military dog. He retired out and my mom took him in. Took a while to get him used to living on a ranch, but Mom did it."

Aaron sighed. "It always does, but not everyone recognizes that patience is key. Nothing good comes overnight." Picking up the leash, he started toward a back portion of the yard and suddenly the dog that didn't want to move was practically dragging the man behind him. As soon as the dog crossed into the smaller kennel area, it was like night and day. His tail started wagging, he stood erect, proud, and bounced around the trainer seeking attention.

"Wow." Preston hadn't meant to say anything.

Sarah, who had remained focused on Samson, nodded. "Other dogs?"

The guy shrugged again. "Not so good."

Which meant Brady might be a problem. She crouched low and opened her palm. The dog crept carefully closer and slowly nibbled the treats from her hand. When the dog leaned into her, Preston could sense Sarah was smiling inside. "Does he have any health issues? Arthritis?"

"None. Clean bill of health." Aaron watched the dog interact with Sarah as she gave him another treat.

Every time the dog leaned into her, she gave him another treat and soon began scratching behind his ears. "I was expecting worse."

"He's a good dog," the man said without taking his eyes away from Samson. "But the slightest change…"

"Yes," Sarah agreed. "I can see that. I have an idea." She handed Preston a few treats and the dog stayed in place, but his gaze tracked the treats and then focused on Preston's hand.

Already squatting near Sarah, Preston opened his hand the way she had. The dog looked back to the man he felt comfortable with, waiting for permission.

"These dogs are always searching for instructions." The trainer lifted his chin at Preston. "Go on," he told the dog and immediately Samson walked over to Preston, a bit more sure of himself.

On a sigh, Sarah pushed to her feet. "Let me see what I can do."

The guy's face broke into a broad smile. "It's getting harder and harder to keep up with the dogs that need retraining. We have someone possibly interested, but we've never worked with her before. If you have someone experienced in mind for this situation, it would be a huge relief for all of us."

Sarah nodded. Preston had the feeling she knew all too well what the man spoke of. "Give me a few days and we'll talk again."

His head bobbing up and down, the man sighed. "I've

got four more coming in next week, if we don't find a placement for Samson..." He let his words hang. Both Sarah and Preston knew what wasn't being said.

Another thirty minutes and they were back in Preston's car and on the road to the Sweet Ranch. Preston could see the wheels turning in Sarah's mind.

"You know," Preston spoke up first. "If you're going to be on the ranch with us for a bit, even if Mom isn't up to it yet, it looked to me like Samson took to you. If they could keep him here until then, and we can figure out how to keep him away from Brady, maybe..."

Sarah nodded.

"What do you think?"

Her gaze shifted from the open road to him, and the muscles in her jaw seemed to hold more tension than he liked. "How do you feel about eloping to Vegas?"

CHAPTER NINE

Even though she'd known she was pretty much out of options, Sarah Sue had spent most of the drive back to the ranch on the phone with different contacts.

"None of that sounds good." Preston pulled onto the ranch drive.

"Your family is Samson's only hope, but I need Alice to be a little more steady on her feet before even suggesting we bring Samson to the ranch."

Once he'd seen the dog, he was much less concerned about his issues, but he had to admit the timing was the pits.

Not for the first time during the drive her phone buzzed. "What've you got for me, Aaron?"

He couldn't quite make out what the voice on the other side said, but her shoulders relaxed and the corners of her mouth lifted slightly.

"Thanks." She disconnected the call and a full smile took over her face. "Two of the dogs Aaron was expecting next week have been placed elsewhere. That buys us some time for Samson."

"Long enough for Mom to heal up?" He came to a stop in front of the house.

She reached for her purse on the floorboard. "Very possibly. We've bought a week at the least, two or three might be doable."

Hopping out of the car, he circled around to her side. "Maybe that's a good sign."

"Sign?" Without hesitation, she slid her hand into his. They'd gotten good at walking and holding hands.

"That everything is going to work out."

She heaved a deep sigh. "I sure as hell hope so."

Inside he could hear women's voices coming from the kitchen and see the light coming from his dad's office. Curious, he headed for the office.

"Hey." Carson looked up from their dad's desk.

"Something wrong?" Carson sat in their dad's office with the same frown he'd had the other day when they all sifted through the books to figure out what was going on.

Carson pushed away from the desk and walked over to the bar. "Checking to see if we overlooked something. An asset hidden somewhere that our beloved foreman missed. See if there's any other way."

Preston could have told him there was nothing. That first night, while everyone else was sleeping, he'd pored over the books. Ray had cleaned them out well and good.

"At dinner, Mom threw out an idea. She wanted all of us to be at the table, but she's worried, so decided against waiting till another time when we're all here."

No sense pointing out they all were worried.

"Anyhow," Carson continued, "she floated finding someone to lease a portion of land for extra income. Pointed out that with the decreased head of cattle we're now running, we could probably spare the space. Of course, that means finding a local rancher who needs more land and that might not happen soon enough."

"Even if we did, it might help buy feed for winter, but it wouldn't be enough to get us out of this mess." Preston knew better than any of them that there was still only one option. The trust.

"Boy, you two sure work fast." Jillian plopped into an overstuffed chair.

On a normal day, Preston would have been asking his sister what the heck she was talking about, but nothing about the last few days had been normal. "Where's Mom?"

Rachel came through the doorway and pointed one finger at the ceiling. "We convinced her to just go to bed early."

"And she listened?" Two dark brows rose high over Carson's deep blue eyes.

Flashing an unusually large grin under the

circumstances, Jillian accepted a cola Carson had poured for her. "Bless Brady."

"What does Brady have to do with it?" He'd hoped to be home early enough to join the family for dinner, but the time with Samson had eaten more of the day than he'd expected. Now he was pedaling fast to keep up.

"That dog is in shepherd mode and Mom is his sheep. When she stood up from the dining room table—slowly— Brady came up beside her and gently nudged her toward the staircase. Once Rachel and I added our two cents, Mom gave up and climbed the steps."

"And Brady?" Preston asked.

"Glued to her side, probably at the foot of the bed now."

"Or across the doorway." Rachel chimed in. "Most shepherds are good protectors too."

"Now that the coast is clear to talk," Jillian leaned forward in her seat and faced her brother, "the whole darn town is talking about you two. Apparently, you've been doing a great job putting on a show. Iris Hathaway has been telling anyone who will listen that Preston is obviously courting Sarah Sue."

"Courting?" Preston hadn't heard that old-fashioned word since he was a kid and his mother made him sit through the old musical *Seven Brides for Seven Brothers*.

"Whatever." Jillian shrugged. "The important thing is, the plan is working."

"Good. Then our running off to Vegas to get married won't surprise anyone." Preston floated the idea that he and Sarah Sue had discussed.

"Vegas?" Carson rubbed the back of his neck. "I understand why you might not want a vow before God church wedding. That makes perfect sense. And I know that Vegas is famous for eloping, but doesn't it seem a bit out of character for both of you?"

"Getting married is out of character for us too," Preston almost snapped at his brother, "but I see your point."

"If you ask me," Rachel turned to Preston, "you've been at this for a whopping three days. No way anyone is going to believe y'all just upped and ran off to get married." When

Preston opened his mouth to protest, his sister held her hand out at him. "I know we're in a hurry, but you need to give it at least a couple of weeks to make it something akin to plausible."

"One week, two weeks." Carson shook his head. "No matter how you slice it, this is going to be pushing our luck."

"What about Oklahoma?" Rachel suggested. When everyone turned to her with confusion, she continued her train of thought. "Unlike Texas, there is no waiting period in Oklahoma. Y'all just drive up to the nearest county seat, pay the fees, and find a judge."

"Mom's going to throw a fit." Jillian sighed. "But Rachel is right, Oklahoma is more believable."

"And who is going to believe that a newly married couple is going to want to rush home and live with their mother?" Carson gaze darted from one sibling to the other.

"Face it." Preston stood. "All of this is a stretch, we have no choice but to go with the flow and pray the bank believes us. In the end, that's all that matters."

"And Mom," the siblings chorused.

"And Mom," Preston repeated, before facing Sarah Sue. "Got any thoughts?"

"I think Oklahoma is more practical than Vegas. We can drive over in a couple of hours and be done with it."

Preston really wished she'd phrased it any other way.

"Maybe stay the night too, make it seem like you at least tried for a honeymoon." Jillian glanced at Sarah Sue for that one.

Sarah Sue turned to Preston. Her gaze seemed to be asking his thoughts. At least he thought that's what she was doing. When he didn't say a word, she sighed. "I'm up for whatever we have to do to save the ranch."

All Preston knew right now is that for someone without a drop of Sweet blood in their veins, or a claim to the family ranch, Sarah Sue was putting an awful lot of her life on the line. The woman was beyond any doubt amazing. "So, it's settled, one week from today, we head off to Oklahoma for a Friday afternoon wedding."

"One week?" Rachel echoed.

Preston eyed Sarah Sue, then faced his sister. "We really can't afford to wait any longer. We can't risk the bank moving forward on foreclosure while we wait to convince the town this is legit."

Jillian sighed. "At least that gives y'all some time to come to your senses."

There was little doubt in Preston's mind that playing husband and wife with Sarah Sue might be too close for comfort to playing with fire. If the last three days had shown him anything, it was that their sweet girl-next-door neighbor had grown up to be one fine woman. And somehow he was going to have to figure out how to keep his hands off of her.

One week. Sarah knew this whole whirlwind courtship would have to be fast, but somehow setting a date made it even more real for her. Almost frighteningly real.

"You'll need witnesses." Carson pushed to his feet. "Even though this isn't technically your big day, it wouldn't look right if at least one of us didn't stand up for you."

A finger in the air, Rachel nodded. "I'll come too."

"Well, foo." Jillian looked ready to stomp her feet and pout. "I can't close the shop on a Friday. Unless I can get Aunt Vicki to cover, but she'll want to know why."

"It's okay." Preston patted his sister's arm. "When I get married for real, you can be a witness."

"Deal." Jillian spun around and hugged her brother.

The sound of someone's cell broke the silent moment. Carson reached for his phone and hit speaker. "You have cell service."

A familiar voice came through the phone. "Came into town for supplies, have a slew of texts from everyone except Kade. Haven't felt this much love since I borrowed your good luck Polo shirt for my date with Mary Jean Gibbons." Their brother Garret chuckled under his breath before shifting to a more serious tone. "What's going on over there?"

Wasn't that a loaded question? If Garret only knew. Carson's gift for brevity had their brother up to date on their mom, their crooked foreman, the money problems, and Preston and Sarah's imminent wedding plans pretty quickly.

"And Mom is definitely okay?" Concern crept into Garret's voice.

"Still sore and slow, but better," Carson kept his voice steady. Their mom would be fine but truth was, everyone was still worried about her—if not her physical health, her emotional state, the one she was trying so hard to hide behind a stiff upper lip.

"You're not lying to me? I could be on a flight home in a couple of hours."

"I'm not lying. Mom will be fine by the time you get home."

"Good." Garret blew out a long sigh that filtered through the room. "In that case, have you all completely lost your minds!"

"Thank heavens." Jillian threw her arms in the air. "Finally, another voice of reason." When both her brothers shot her a pointed glare, Jillian dropped her arms to her side and shoulder's deflated, sighed. "Never mind."

The next twenty minutes were spent convincing Garret they hadn't all lost their minds, and no he did not need to cut his summer vacation short and fly home to talk some sense into them. Although Preston wondered if having one more son home wouldn't help cheer up his mother; the next couple of weeks were going to be hard enough, one more person having to keep up the illusion was more stress than any of them needed.

Disconnecting the call and slipping the phone into his shirt pocket, Carson leaned back in his father's chair. "Well, that could have been worse."

"Kade's going to have the same reaction when he hears." Jillian waved her hands at the heads turned in her direction. "Just saying."

For a long few minutes, no one said a word. What was

there to say?

"She's right," Preston spoke up. "No sense in stressing Kade out. For now, let's spare him all the details."

Multiple heads bobbed. Rachel nibbled on her lower lip a moment longer before blowing out a sigh and nodding her agreement.

"All right then. Now that we've got Garret and Kade settled, we have a few more people to include." Preston crossed the room and stopped in front of Sarah. "Shall we go to your house and have a chat with your father?"

Sarah let out a deep sigh. "I've been thinking about that."

"And?" Preston urged.

"Dad can keep a secret, but what if he doesn't agree with us and feels obligated to tell your mother? This isn't quite the same as doctor patient confidentiality." She had no idea what was harder, pretending that she wasn't attracted to Preston, or lying to her father for the sake of the ranch.

One hand raked his fingers through his hair before extending his arms and taking one of Sarah's hands in each of his. "It's your call. Whatever you want, I'm on board."

Did he have to make things so easy? Be so cooperative and understanding? Why was this man the only man she'd ever dated who was practical, level-headed, and thoughtful? *Dated?* She hadn't really dated Preston, she was just marrying him.

"You okay?" Preston held onto her hands and frowned.

"I don't know what to do."

"About your father?"

Yeah. Sure. "Yes." Pulling away, she sighed. This whole enterprise was too important to risk the secret getting out. "Like it or not, if your mom stays in the dark, my dad stays in the dark."

His head cocked to one side. "You sure?"

No. "Yes." As sure as she could be in this crazy situation.

★

"I can't put my finger on it, but something is off." Alice Sweet had her sister on speaker phone.

"What do you mean off?"

"Well, why now?" Alice said.

Vicki sighed on the other end. "You really do like looking a gift horse in the mouth, don't you? You know as well as anyone else, imminent danger brings couples together. Haven't you ever seen the movie *Speed*?"

"That's when the couple is in imminent danger, not me."

"Do you have any idea how much you scared the heck out of everyone with that fall?"

Her sister was right. She could see the fear and worry in each and every one of her children's faces, even now. "I know."

"And now, they're waiting for you to show signs of improvement. Those two have been friends since Sarah Sue could talk. Makes perfectly good sense to me, now that she's home that is."

"I suppose you're right. I'm just being foolish. Ray has left me doubting everything."

"Any word from the sheriff on his whereabouts?"

"Nothing." That was bothering Alice as much as the thefts and embezzlement. Where the hell was that thieving foreman and all the other hands? More importantly—what if he came back for more?

"I can hear the worry wheels spinning in your head."

Some days it was uncanny how well she and her sisters knew each other. How they could read each other. And every minute of every day, she was so very thankful for them.

"Now on to bigger and more important things," her sister continued.

"What could be more important than my son dating my next-door neighbor?"

"The corn hole tournament. Liz and I have decided we're going to enter."

"I thought you two considered competing a conflict of interest?"

"That was before. Now we want that prize money. For you."

"Y'all don't have to do that." Her heart squeezed with appreciation at their desire to help.

"No, we don't. But we want to." Vicki's words hung for a long minute. "No arguments."

Her sister was right. With the mess Ray had left her, she was going to need every penny she could get her hands on. Saving almost a week's salary for all the missing hands, she was able to make a payment on the loan. It wasn't enough to address all the missed payments, interest, and penalties, but the bank seemed to take it to heart that she was trying. Probably didn't hurt that the same bank had been handling the family trust for a couple of hundred years with a tidy sum in the account.

The trust. If only she could borrow against that. Then she could get production up and running the way Charlie had wanted and start paying off all their debts. "Oh, Charlie. Why does life have to be difficult without you?"

CHAPTER TEN

What was that old expression? *The days are long but the years are short.* Well, not this past week. The days flew by. Preston and Sarah had gallivanted around town every day, indulged in homemade ice cream at the Creamery; he even licked the melting drops from her cone before giving her a peck on the lips for all to see. They'd played more corn hole, and even beat a few of the people who had stopped to watch. At one point they'd gone to the playground and he'd pushed her on the swings. He felt like a teenager crushing on the prom queen as Sarah laughed and giggled and smiled up at him. And of course, they'd eaten out pretty much every other night, and when they didn't come to town to eat, they ate with his mom or her dad. The way their parents kept grinning at the two of them he wished he didn't have to go through all the subterfuge, but the situation was what it was. At least the stress of bringing Samson home was off Sarah Sue's plate. That one prospect Aaron had mentioned to them had been green-lighted to take the dog home.

Now he stood in front of his dresser and could barely button his shirt. Never in his life could he remember being so nervous. In a few more hours, he and Sarah Sue would be standing in front of a judge and would become man and wife. His fingers slipped and he almost popped a button.

"Here. Let me." Carson brushed Preston's hands aside and began lining up the buttons. "You'd think this was for real."

"It is," Preston snapped.

"Not technically."

"It's legally binding. How much more technical do you

want to get?"

"Okay. It's real but temporary." Carson finished the last button and patted his brother's arm. "All set. Rachel is almost done drying her hair and then we can go pick up Sarah."

"Where did you tell Mom we're going?"

"I didn't. Thought that was your place."

Preston nodded. "I've been kicking around possibilities for the last week and have failed to come up with any idea that is merely skirting the truth rather than an outright lie."

"Well, I have a job and you have a job so leaving the house isn't that odd."

"No."

"Why don't you just say you have a business deal out of town? After all, this is a business arrangement of sorts, then Mom won't be surprised that you're not coming home till tomorrow."

"Right. Good point." Taking one last look in the mirror, he wondered if he should have worn a different shirt. Then again, what difference did it make?

"You go ahead and pick up Sarah." Carson took a step back. "I'll follow you with Rachel."

Preston agreed with that plan. Since Carson and Rachel were returning home after the wedding, taking two cars was the only practical thing to do. Twenty minutes later, he'd said his goodbyes to his mother, Sarah's dad had already left for the day, and now his bride sat in the passenger side of his car. Carson and Rachel would be leaving a respectable thirty minutes after him. Lord, he hoped this all worked out. He'd already filled out the paperwork for the bank trustee. First thing Monday morning he and Sarah would present the forms and marriage license and say their prayers that no one laughed in their faces.

He didn't know why, but without thinking, he reached over across the console and took hold of Sarah's hand. When she squeezed back, he laced his fingers with hers and wondered if he would feel any differently if this was all for real.

Nearly halfway to the courthouse, still holding hands,

Sarah sighed. "Ever wonder why it always feels like it takes longer going somewhere than returning home?"

A small chuckle tickled his throat. He supposed equating the anticipation with walking the plank would not be appropriate. "The unknown. Coming home is always familiar."

"Familiar," she echoed. "Makes sense."

It also explained why holding hands felt so natural. After almost two weeks of performing for the town, everything about Sarah Sue felt familiar and natural. Maybe he was being nervous about nothing.

The car in park, Preston glanced over at Sarah Sue, their fingers still intertwined. "Last chance to change your mind," he teased.

Her smile seemed shakier than usual and the extra few moments it took for her to react had him thinking this may be as far is it all went. Squeezing his fingers, she pulled her hand away, stiffened her smile, and sucked in a deep breath. "Let's go save a ranch."

A car zoomed into the space beside them. Rachel popped out of the car and waved an arm. "This place is adorable. I think that gazebo will be perfect for the ceremony."

Sarah turned and nodded, Carson raised a brow at his brother. Preston agreed, Rachel was a little too happy for a fake ceremony.

"Oh." Rachel stretched out her other arm. "One for you, one for me."

Sarah's gaze dropped to the two small bouquets of fresh flowers in his sister's hands. A hand steadier than his own reached for a bouquet and then she took a slow sniff. A more genuine smile took over her face. "Thank you. This was sweet."

"I've never been a maid of honor before but I did my best." Handing her bouquet to her brother, Rachel rummaged through her purse. "Here's my grandmother's engraved handkerchief. If you put it in your pocket, that will be the something old. I'm considering the flowers new. This is the borrowed." Reaching behind her neck, she unclasped a simple gold chain with an open heart charm dangling and hung it on Sarah's neck, then stripped a gaudy silver and blue bracelet from her wrist. "Here's Mom's souvenir bracelet from Coney Island. Dad took her to New York on their honeymoon. The thing is cheap as all get out but Mom loves it. I figure it'll work for good luck and something blue."

Sarah Sue flung her arms around his sister. "Thank you. This is seriously sweet of you."

Tipping her head and grinning, Rachel shrugged. "Wouldn't want to fail my first time out."

"All right." Carson cleared his throat. "Let's get the paperwork rolling. The officiate texted that he'll meet us at the gazebo in fifteen minutes."

Fifteen minutes and the three hundred and sixty-five day countdown would begin. Only fifteen minutes and life as they all knew it was about to be turned on its head.

For the life of her, Sarah couldn't decide if Rachel adding all the touches of an actual wedding made things better or worse. It only took a few minutes to fill out the paperwork and for the clerk to give them an old-fashioned typed marriage license. Reminding herself every few moments to smile, she also had to loosen her grip on the flowers every time her fingers began to cramp from the tight hold.

Without thinking, her hand fingered the heart hanging from her neck. A smile pulled at the corners of her mouth. Rachel was so very thoughtful. Her gaze lifted to meet Preston's; he'd been watching her.

His eyes softened and his lips curled in a smile. "Last chance to change your mind."

A car door slammed, and a bushy-haired man with a mustache to match waved at them.

Her gaze shifted back to Preston and she took in a calming deep breath. "I was just going to ask you the same thing."

"No need to ask which is the happy couple." The man came to a stop in front of them. "Always a good sign when eyes sparkle with love."

Carson coughed so hard, Rachel had to slap him on his back before staring daggers at him.

"Papers in order?"

With a nod, Preston handed the new license over for the man to peruse.

"Very well. The rings?"

Preston began patting his pockets. "I don't need one, but…" a frown deepened between his brows.

"You gave it to me." Rolling his eyes, Carson reached into his pocket and produced a simple gold band.

"Yes. Right." Preston sighed and the officiate just smiled.

Sarah reached into her purse and pulled out a small velvet pouch. An equally simple, but much larger band dropped onto her palm and without a word, she handed it over to Rachel.

"You got me a ring?" Preston's voice was soft and low and vibrated through her, all the way to her toes.

"Wasn't I supposed to?"

Not till his lips curved into a lazy smile did she truly relax. For the first time since they stood on the corner, the night his apartment caught fire and she made up her mind to do this, she was completely at peace and completely sure they could make this work.

Curling her arm into his elbow, Preston turned them to face the judge. "Let's get this show on the road."

The next thing she knew, she was facing Preston, their hands clasped, and each was repeating the words the officiate fed them. Her hand tingled as Preston slowly eased the single band onto her finger. A moment later, and she was shoving a different gold band over Preston's knuckle, praying the ring fit, smiling with delight when the wedding band settled comfortably onto his finger.

"By the powers vested in me by the state of Oklahoma, I pronounce you husband and wife. You may now kiss the bride."

They'd kissed before. They'd had to for appearance's sake. Always quick and brief and just for show. This time, Preston's lips came down on hers, slowly, carefully, and so very sweetly. The air warmed around her and the ground beneath her feet seemed to shift. The touch lasted just long enough to convince anyone looking, but not long enough for Sarah's liking. Probably for the best.

A few handshakes and hugs of congratulations, all for the benefit of the officiate who signed the paperwork then quickly said his goodbyes and wished them every happiness. The same loud slamming of a car door announced his departure.

Spinning about, Rachel leveled her gaze with Preston, then over to Sarah Sue. "On behalf of Mom, Dad, and the ranch, thank you for doing this."

"Yes." Carson turned to Sarah Sue. "We'll never be able to repay you."

All she could manage was a nod. When Preston squeezed her hand, whether for support or adding his thanks, she was able to add a hopefully steady smile. "That ranch feels as much a home to me as my dad's house."

Blinking back watery eyes, Rachel took a step in retreat. "Yes. Well, I guess this is it. I hate to marry and run, but we need to get back before Mom notices anything is different."

Preston nodded. "Of course. Thanks for the assist."

Slapping his brother on the back, Carson took a step back before turning around and hugging his brother hard. "See you tomorrow."

Not till Carson and Rachel's car pulled out of its parking spot did Preston take a step forward. "Hungry?"

"Not really." As soon as the words were out of her mouth, she realized if they didn't go eat that meant the only other place to go was to check into their room.

"Popcorn?"

"What?"

"How about popcorn? I'd suggest we do a little sightseeing but I'm pretty sure from where we're standing we can see the whole town. On the other hand, if we head to our hotel, we can get a large bowl of popcorn and binge a few good movies."

The butterflies in her stomach stopped fluttering and a smile touched her lips. "I love popcorn."

Small-town Oklahoma was not known for luxury accommodations, but Preston chose the nicest hotel he could find. After a quick stop at a local grocery for popcorn, sodas, and a few miscellaneous snacks, checking in had been easy. So far, the closest thing to a boutique hotel had kept all of its charm. Even the old-fashioned key fob with the logo on one side and room number on the other was cute. What wasn't so cute was the sight awaiting him at the room's open door.

He'd booked a double room. The photos had shown rooms with two double beds. This room had one king-size bed. No chairs and no extra space.

"Oh." Sarah came to a stop beside him. "It's, um, very pretty."

Not the first words that came to his mind. "There are supposed to be two beds."

"Oh," she repeated softly.

Shaking his head, he walked to the phone on a nearby table and punched the number for the front desk. A moment later the woman who answered explained that they were fully booked for the night and there were no other options. "Do you have a rollaway bed?" The lady's answer wasn't anymore helpful. Setting the handle back into the cradle, he blew out a sigh. "Looks like this is it."

Glancing about, Sarah spotted the luggage rack in one corner and slowly crossing the room, set her bag down on it. Her back to him, he could see her shoulders rise and fall with a deep breath before she opened her bag and pulled out a small toiletry kit and then clutching it to her chest, turned to face him. "Which side of the bed do you want?"

His gaze darted to the large bed. "I, uh, don't know." Right now if she asked him for his full-given name, he'd probably stumble over it.

"I'd rather sleep on the side closest to the bathroom. I get cold easily when the a/c kicks on."

"Of course." Searching the closet, he pulled out an extra blanket and set it on her side of the bed. At least it was a king. If they each stayed to their side, he could probably sleep two more people between them. Skinny people. For a brief moment, he wondered how stupid would it look if he were to stack pillows between them. Images of an old movie he'd watched as a kid with his mom flashed through his mind. The couple had strung a blanket between them. Even at a young age Preston had thought it rather stupid, but suddenly, adding any extra barrier seemed like a good idea.

The bathroom door squeaked open and Sarah strolled out wearing Pepto Bismol pink sweatpants and a turquoise sweatshirt. She reminded him of a popular bottle of sunscreen and had to bite back a smile.

"I get cold easily." Moving quickly, she dropped the bag and her clothes into the suitcase and hurried to the bed, pausing at the sight of the blanket. Her head turned to face him and a smile seemed to tease the corners of her mouth. "Thank you."

"You're welcome."

Yanking the covers back, she quickly crawled into her side of the bed and glanced at the clock on the end table.

Fully clothed, he sat on his side of the bed and picked up the remote control. A few clicks and he scrolled onto a movie channel. "Have you seen the new *Top Gun* movie?"

Pillows propped behind her, she shook her head. "I wanted to, but never got around to it."

He nodded. "Tom Cruise it is."

Another few minutes and they were both settled in, a bowl of popcorn between them and Tom Cruise up to his same cocky antics. Sarah cracked up laughing as often as she buried her face in her hands. More than once he'd been tempted to inch closer and curl her into his side—not a good idea. By the end of the movie, they'd settled into an old comedy with Elvis Presley and a dancer whose name he didn't recognize. By the end of that movie, Sarah had fallen asleep, snuggled under the covers. Flipping channels, he opted for the most boring movie he could find. Maybe, if there was a God in heaven, he could drift off to sleep and not notice he was in bed with a beautiful woman. And maybe some day soon, pigs would fly.

CHAPTER ELEVEN

Preston pulled up to the ranch house and threw the car into park. Last night, after Sarah had fallen asleep, even though he was still wide awake, he slipped under the covers and turned off the television. After an hour of flipping back and forth and punching his pillow, he finally gave up and turned the television back on. He had no idea when he fell asleep, but he woke up with a warm, soft woman tucked into his side and resisted the urge to kiss her awake. Instead, he slid out of bed and took a long, cool shower. For the last hour of the drive, he'd quietly repeated to himself that this whole crazy idea wasn't a mistake. Too bad he didn't believe it, but here they were. "Are you ready?"

Closing her eyes a moment, Sarah nodded and looked over at him. "Do you think they'll believe us?"

"We have the license to prove it. My concern is they're going to kill us for not including them long before the bank ever hands over the money."

"Yeah." She blew out a deep sigh. "Guess I'm as ready as I can be."

"Wait here a second." He hurried around the front of the vehicle and opened her door. Leaning in, he couldn't help himself and gave her a brief kiss on the lips. "For luck. And in case anyone's watching."

Before Sarah had fully descended, tail wagging, Brady came rushing up to them. "Hi there, handsome." Sarah leaned over to scratch the dog's ears. "You sure know how to make a girl feel welcome."

The dog leaned back on his haunches and Preston would have wagered the ranch that the animal had smiled at her. Did German Shepherds smile? Ever?

As she straightened, the front door opened and his mother appeared in the doorway. She'd come a long way from the bloody and bruised woman of just a couple of weeks ago, but the sadness in her eyes still grabbed him by the throat. Day after day she'd thrown out impossible ideas of how to save the ranch. Of course, none would make a dent in the debt. This was why he and Sarah had to fool his mother, it was the only way to help her. The only way. Not a mistake.

Carefully holding Sarah's hand, he gave a gentle squeeze and with his free hand waved at his mother. Her gaze immediately dropped to their clasped hands as they crossed the gravel drive and stepped onto the porch. "Hi, Mom."

Alice Sweet smiled at her son. "How'd the trip go?"

"Very well." Even though there was no reason, he could feel heat taking over his face. Stepping forward, he kissed his mom on the cheek and then quickly retreating to Sarah's side, took hold of her hand again.

The sparkle that had been missing from his mother's eyes seemed to be flickering faintly. "It's nice to see you again, Sarah Sue."

Now or never. He sucked in a deep breath. "As of last night, that would be Mrs. Sarah Sue Sweet."

His mother's eyes rounded, exposing a swath of white around dark blue eyes that resembled his. Her gaze darted from him to Sarah Sue and back. "You wouldn't tease an old lady, would you?"

"You are not old." He rolled his eyes and then, realizing his mother was anxiously waiting, he shook his head and grabbing hold of Sarah's wrist, held up her left hand.

Before he could react, his mother flung herself at Sarah Sue, her arms folding around his new bride's petite frame. "I knew it. Deep down I've always known it." Still strangling Sarah Sue, his mom grinned like the Cheshire cat. "I just wasn't so sure y'all would ever figure it out."

Caught in a tight bear hug, Sarah glanced over her mother-in-law's shoulder and flashed a stiff smile at

Preston. This was not the reaction he'd expected. Not that he was sure what he actually expected, but total delight and acceptance was not anywhere on the list, never mind at the top.

"Y'all going to come inside or are you planning on growing roots out there?" In a pair of mud splattered jeans and a button-down shirt with sleeves rolled up, his sister Rachel stood grinning from the front porch.

His mom sprang back and rubbing her hands together, spun about to Preston and pulled him into a tight squeeze, and up on her tippy toes, whispered, "I'm so very happy for you."

Shaking off his confusion, he held on to his mother. "I love you, Mom."

"If someone doesn't hurry up and get in here," Carson now stood beside their sister, "I'm going to fix lunch."

"Oh no." His mom stepped back. "I'm going to fix every favorite thing for you, and you're going to tell me every single detail of the wedding." She turned to Sarah. "Of course, we'll have your dad over to celebrate." A deep frown suddenly made itself at home above his mom's brow. "Does he know?"

Sarah Sue shook her head. "We came here first. Dad won't be home for a few hours and I wanted to tell him in person."

"Of course you do." His mom looped her arm with Sarah Sue and began walking toward the house with Brady dancing around them.

Preston couldn't say who was happier over the news, his mother or Brady. Maybe the world really had turned on its head.

"We'll have a nice lunch, and you can tell me all about the wedding." She craned her neck to look at Preston following beside them. "I'll forgive you for not inviting me, but," she looked up at her other two children, "anyone else pull a stunt like this and I'll tan your hides."

"Yes, ma'am," Rachel and Carson echoed.

On the porch, his mom finally released her hold on Sarah Sue and still grinning wider than he'd ever seen, she hurried into the house.

As he passed his sister, she shrugged at him while Carson mouthed, "That went better than I expected."

Exactly the same thing Preston had been thinking. Remembering he had a part to play, he quickly took hold of Sarah's hand and together they followed his siblings into the house.

Standing at the sink, hugging a bowl against her midriff and stirring the ingredients together, his mom shook her head before waving a cream slathered spoon. "What I don't understand is why elope? Why couldn't we have had a regular wedding?" Suddenly, Alice Sweet's eyes rounded wider than before. "Unless...."

"No." Preston knew exactly where her mind had gone. He suspected a lot of folks in town would think the same thing. "Sarah is not pregnant."

To his surprise, that made his mom sigh before the smile returned. "As much as I would love having a little one to love on, I'm glad to hear y'all simply came to your senses."

That much he still wasn't sure about.

An entire year of this just might kill her. Despite Alice Sweet's insistence that she didn't need help, Sarah Sue pushed to her feet and turned to Preston. "Would you like something to drink?"

"I can get it."

"No." She smiled. "I'm up."

"Is it too early for a beer?" he teased.

Instinctively, she leaned over and kissed his temple. "I'm sure it's five o'clock somewhere." When she turned toward the fridge, she spotted Alice grinning at them. With every step, all she could think was *a whole year*.

"So," Alice poured the mixture into a pie tin, "what now?"

"Now?" Preston fiddled with a napkin on the table.

"Is there going to be a honeymoon? Where are you going to live? How long do I have to wait to be a grandmother?"

"Mom." Preston sounded like a mortified teen. "No time for a real honeymoon. There's too much work to be done here."

"We can manage without you for a little while."

"You might, but my office won't take kindly to my disappearing on them."

Sarah knew Preston hadn't told his mother that his bosses weren't overjoyed with his new schedule. Taking time off for a pretend honeymoon was out of the question. One interesting twist to the awkward honeymoon night had been the conversation between movies. Something about sharing a bed and a bag of popcorn made sharing fears and dreams easier. Though she'd refrained from mentioning just how scared she was that walking away a year from now was not going to be as easy as she'd expected.

"Okay," his mom nodded, "no honeymoon." She slid the pie tins into the oven and closed the door. "Did you find an apartment?"

Preston glanced at Sarah. "Uh, not exactly."

Returning to the countertop where his mother appeared to be making every dessert that Preston had ever loved, Alice Sweet leaned against the counter. "What exactly?"

"Until we find someplace else," he reached over and grabbed Sarah's hand again, "which may be a while, we thought Sarah would move into my old room with me."

"Are you nuts?" His mother pushed away from the sink, shaking her head. "That room looks the same as it did when you were in college. I mean, I love all your trophies, but that's no place to bring home a bride."

He shrugged. "It will do."

"No, it won't." Alice turned toward the sink and pulled another bowl out of the cupboard. "You'll take my room for now. I'll talk to Clint, see what we can do to arrange for something more suitable."

"Mom." Again, Preston practically whined.

Her hand up, palm out, Alice Sweet shot her son a glare

that Sarah Sue hadn't seen since they were all little kids. "No argument. As soon as we're done eating, we'll start moving everything around."

Preston went to open his mouth and Sarah simply squeezed his hand. His gaze immediately swiveled in her direction and she very softly shook her head. While Sarah was not Alice Sweet's daughter, she was smart enough to recognize that 'because Mom said so,' tone and knew that arguing now would only make things worse.

Peppered with questions from her new mother-in-law about the proposal, the wedding, and everything imaginable about their courtship, with the help of Carson and Rachel, Sarah Sue and Preston pretty much gave one of the best performances of their lives. They smiled at each other, occasionally touched hands between bites of their grilled cheese lunch with Alice's deep-fried potato chips, and every so often, Sarah Sue found herself almost believing everything was real about this charade.

"All right." Preston's mom stood from the kitchen table, a dish in each hand. "Clean up in here can wait. Time to get your new room ready." Alice paused at her son's side and running the back of her hand down his cheek, smiled at him. "I know you two will be as happy as your dad and I were, maybe happier." With a sweet smile, she sashayed up the stairs.

"I don't want to kick her out of her room." Preston faced Sarah. "It doesn't seem right."

"I know how you feel, but it's what she wants." Sarah felt just as awful about moving into Alice's room as Preston did, but she didn't know what else to do. "Overall, I'm pretty stunned at how well she's taking all this. I really thought she was going to read us the riot act. If switching rooms makes her even happier, then what's the harm?"

His eyes momentarily squeezed shut, Preston blinked and blew out a sigh. "I hate this."

In her mind, Sarah understood he meant lying to his mother, but her gut clenched nonetheless at the idea that being with her could be so distasteful.

"Hey." His finger under her chin, he lifted her face and

leveled his gaze with hers. "I didn't mean that the way it sounded. I just didn't realize lying to my mother would be this hard."

There was no point mentioning she felt the same about her father, or how much she worried about his reaction to the news. "I know."

The intensity in his gaze had Sarah's pulse kicking up a notch. Even though there was no one standing around watching, for just a second, she thought he was going to lean in and kiss her. She almost closed her eyes in anticipation when she heard the sound of someone clearing their throat.

"You two going to stay in the kitchen all day?" Alice Sweet stood in the doorway grinning.

"Coming, Mom." Smiling back at his mother, Preston took hold of Sarah Sue's hand and leaned against her. "Looks like we're getting a bigger room."

We. Somehow, she was pretty sure the Taj Mahal wouldn't be big enough for her heart to hide for the next three hundred and sixty-four nights.

CHAPTER TWELVE

His mom was definitely in a very good mood. Preston's mother had turned on the stereo, loud enough to be heard through the whole house, and had set the radio in her room to the same station. They were being bombarded by stereophonic sound from all sides.

"I finally have good reason to clean out your father's side of the closet." Alice Sweet dropped a handful of shirts, hangers and all, into a box. "I've had these boxes stacked in the closet for ages. Guess this was the motivation I needed."

Preston stood in the doorway to his parents' bedroom. "Mom, we don't have to do this." He was beginning to sound like the proverbial broken record.

His mom lifted her head and leveled her gaze with his, a bright smile on her face. "It's time. And your father's side is already for your clothes. I'll move mine into yours and then Sarah can have my closet. Perfect."

Reluctantly, Preston nodded. "Perfect."

As he and Sarah Sue carried armfuls of clothes from his closet, his mother pulled out a drawer and carried it over to Preston's room. In the closet, he hung a few pairs of pants and arms full, Sarah sidled up beside him. An oldie song came on the radio and Sarah's head started bobbing as she one by one hung shirts on the rod. By the time her arms were free, Preston was feeling the rhythm as well. On impulse, he took hold of her hand and twirled her in place.

Sarah Sue let out a cute girlish giggle and he swirled her into his arms and swayed left then right, her laughter bubbling over.

How could he resist? He twirled her around again and dropped her into a deep dip.

Laughter filled the room and when he lifted her up, she spun around into his arms.

Staring down at her, he was overwhelmed at the urge to pull her in even closer and kiss her, really kiss her. Instead, his mom appeared in the doorway.

"Oh." Alice Sweet stopped, her smile impossibly brighter. "Sorry. I just wanted to put this drawer back and grab another."

Both his sister and brother, each carrying an armful of folded clothes, came to a stop behind their mother.

"This is no time for a traffic jam." Carson shifted around his mother. "Mom says these go in the drawers she's been emptying."

"Ditto." Rachel appeared on their mother's other side. "No one said a thing about a dance break."

Still grinning, their mother crossed the room, shoved the empty drawer back into the dresser and spun around. "Back to work, everyone."

Another few moments and they were all traipsing back and forth across the hall, moving clothes around, stripping bed sheets, and with each crossing there was a little more swing in everyone's step.

Content with the progress they'd made so quickly in swapping out bedrooms, Alice took a minute to run downstairs and check on the desserts she'd set in the oven.

The back door cracked open and Clint, the lone ranch hand left, stomped his feet on the mat and held his hat in his hands. "Afternoon, Miss Alice." He paused, his head cocked slightly to one side, eyes narrowed. "You're looking awfully spry today."

"Spry?" She shook her head. "Why does that make me feel twenty years older than I am?"

"Sorry, ma'am." He slapped his hat against his thigh.

"Ma'am. Oh dear, make that thirty years."

Poor Clint actually blushed. His feet shuffled from side

to side, and slowly he fully lifted his head to level his gaze with hers. "I'm sorry to have to say this. There's a section of fence down in the south pasture. From what I can see, we're missing about a dozen cows."

Her breath caught in her throat as she managed to squeak out, "Ray?"

"I don't know, but I think not. It looks like the fence just gave out."

"Gave out," she muttered. Even though she needed for more things to fall apart like she needed another fall on the barbed wire; at least it was way better than cut by that sniveling, thieving, former foreman, Ray.

"I rigged the fence for now, but if I could get one of your boys to give me a hand, we can find the missing cattle, then I can fix the fence right."

Fix it right. They were so tight on money at the moment that she could barely afford to buy toilet paper, never mind much needed supplies. "About that."

"Please don't go there again."

"There?"

"About my pay. I told you, a roof over my head and three square meals a day is all I need till the ranch is on sound footing."

And there was that too. Would this place ever be on sound footing again? Along with the other ranch hands whose salary she'd been able to use toward loan payments, Clint had refused his paycheck and insisted she add it the payment. Something she hadn't intended to make a long-term arrangement, but apparently that was her only hand's intent. She could see some of their older hands who had been with them for decades doing something like that, but the good guys were all gone. One by one the cowhands who had spent years on the payroll had given some excuse or other for moving on, and, of course, their replacements were much younger and hired by Ray. No doubt the former ranch hands leaving, like all her other cattle trouble, had been orchestrated or manipulated by the crooked foreman. Now, Clint was their most recent hire. The man hadn't been here but a few months before Ray and the rest of the hands slithered into the night, and yet, he seemed to have a loyalty to the ranch that had no rhyme or reason. Did it? She shook her head and reminded herself why she had reason to smile. "Not today."

"Excuse me?"

"Preston and Sarah Sue are married."

"Hitched?"

Her cheeks hurting from so much smiling, she bobbed her head. "Hitched."

One side of his mouth tipped upward in a hint of a smile. "Congratulations, Miss Alice. Miss Sarah Sue is a nice gal. I've only met her a time or two, but anyone can see she's good people."

"Yes, she is. It's about time something positive happened to this place." Losing Charlie had almost broken her, finding out what Ray had done only made things worse, but today, today all was well with the universe.

"I guess the cattle and fence can keep till morning."

Shaking her head, she waved a finger at him as if he were a small child. "You're not working on the Lord's day, Clint."

"No, ma'am." His eyes widened suddenly. "I mean, Miss Alice."

His sudden backpedaling of the polite name that had made her feel horribly old a few moments ago, now made her want to laugh. "Join us for supper? A celebration of sorts."

Heavy boot steps came down the stairs and Clint lifted his gaze in time to see Carson coming toward the kitchen with a full laundry basket in hand.

"Thank you for the offer," Clint took a step in retreat and shoved his hat on his head, "but it's been a long day."

Without a word, Alice nodded and watched the door close behind the one man who she was learning to trust even if he wasn't family.

"Was it something I said?" Carson dropped the basket on the kitchen table.

Staring at the back door, Alice shook her head and turned to smile at her son. "We lost a fence in the south pasture, and a few cows. We'll deal with it Monday."

Carson's brow shot up. Ranch work didn't take holidays. Even for the Lord's day, cattle needed to be tended, and problems needed to be handled. Only today, shoving her doubts aside, she was taking a break to celebrate a happy union. Even if it killed everyone.

"You look absolutely ridiculous." Sarah Sue did her best not to laugh out loud at Preston in a red velvet Mexican sombrero.

"Hey, when you're thirteen years old and the sales girl has big brown eyes and lashes that cast a shadow across her cheeks, the hat is a bargain."

"I bet." The stacks of boxes at the bottom of Preston's closet were a regular treasure trove. They'd sorted through baseball hats, basketball trophies, team signed footballs and baseballs, and a few things she couldn't quite figure out. But the sombrero was the most laughable.

"Need more boxes?" Carson stood in the doorway of what until this morning had been his mom's room.

"Trash bags make more sense." Preston pointed to the stack of old trophies, then moving to the bed, waved his arm over a multitude of drawers sprawled across the bed. "It's a safe bet I am never fitting in my sophomore year basketball shirt."

"Considering you're about six inches taller than you were then, I'd say that's an affirmative." Carson shook his head at the drawers.

The music still playing, though not as loudly, a song Sarah had never heard began and soon she found herself tapping her toes.

"Like Bill Withers?" Preston's mom came in carrying a large wicker basket.

"Who?" three voices echoed.

From behind his mom, Rachel rolled her eyes. "Don't let them get to you, Mom. They have no taste."

A toothy smile on her face that made her eyes twinkle, Alice Sweet bopped—there was no other word for it—over to her son and taking his hand, pulled him out into the middle of the bedroom floor. Without skipping a beat, Carson twirled his mother in place and then fell into a dance step that reminded her of an old Fred Astaire or Gene Kelly movie. Another chorus of "Lovely Day" began and with a shrug, Preston extended his hand to Sarah. "Shall we?"

"I don't think I know how," she chuckled.

"Sure you do. It's like a glorified two step." As his brother had done, Preston spun Sarah into his arms and then began twirling and swinging her back and forth.

She knew from her prom that the man had rhythm, and the brief spin by the closet a short while ago showed he could still move, but she had no idea he was this good of a dancer. She felt like Ginger Rogers whirling around the room. Every time he twirled her into his arms, she couldn't help but giggle with delight.

Somewhere she'd missed Jillian arriving and now dancing with her sister. This was some serious fun. Good thing there was plenty of space for everyone. Another tune came on, and she suspected by the beat, it was the same singer. No one showed any signs of stopping or returning to sorting out the two rooms, and Sarah didn't care, she was enjoying herself too much.

Smiling, Doc Conroy knocked on the doorframe. "I followed the music. Can I join the party?"

As much fun as she was having, Sarah couldn't help but tense at her father's arrival.

"It'll be okay," Preston pulled her closer and whispered into her ear. "Might as well get it over with."

Squeezing her eyes shut, she took in a deep breath and nodded. He was right. No sense slowly tugging at a Band-Aid—just rip it off and ignore the pain.

The song eased to an end and Preston tucked Sarah into his side. "Doc. We have something we'd like to share with you."

Her father leveled his gaze with Sarah Sue before shifting his attention back to Preston. "If you're about to tell me you need help straightening out this mess, you're on your own."

Preston chuckled. "No, sir." Lacing his fingers with hers, Preston smiled at her father. "But, as of yesterday afternoon, Sarah and I are married."

Brows drawn together, her father repeated, "Married?"

Sarah's mouth had gone so dry, she couldn't have opened it to form words if she'd pried it open with a crow bar.

"Isn't it wonderful news!" Alice Sweet spun in place and opening her arms wide, pulled Sarah's dad into a tight hug. "We're all family now."

From where Sarah stood, she saw her dad's stiff shoulders ease and then slowly step back and turn to face Sarah. "Really?"

All Sarah could do was nod. This was the moment she'd been dreading.

Her father tipped his head to one side, studying his daughter.

Preston pulled Sarah in closer to his side and letting go of her hand, slung his arm around her shoulder.

The gesture must have been what her father was looking for because his curious gaze shifted to a twinkling eyed smile and he leapt forward, pulling his daughter into the tightest squeeze. "I would have preferred to walk you down the aisle, but that's okay, we'll have a nice big reception. I love you, baby." Pulling away, he smiled at them. "I couldn't be happier."

And *that* was exactly what Sarah had been so afraid of.

"Nothing went the way I expected it to today." Preston untucked his shirt and sank onto the foot of the bed.

"Ditto." Hands clasped in her lap, Sarah Sue sat about a foot away from him. "I knew the town gossips had briefly expected us to get together—that is after all how this whole idea came to be. But my father? Your mother? How did we miss they've been expecting us to get together too?"

"I don't know." Just about everything today had been surreal. For starters, Preston was now a married man. Then, the shock, surprise, and even disbelief he'd expected from at least one of the parents, if not both of them, never happened. "You'd think they'd have had at least a few questions."

"Yep." Sarah Sue sighed.

"When your dad shook my hand and then pulled me into a hug to welcome me to the family, I almost broke down then and there to tell him the truth."

"I know what you mean. Every time dad smiled at me with so much pride and happiness in his eyes, I wanted to shout out to forget that we'd said anything." A soft smile teased her lips. "Though it was fun dancing. I haven't danced with my dad since I was in high school."

Preston nodded. After supper his mom turned the music back on and they'd all danced. His aunts had joined them for dinner and once all the squealing and cheering had died down and dinner had been consumed, the whole family danced for hours. He was almost tired enough to fall dead asleep. Almost.

"Mind if I use the bathroom first?" Sarah pushed to her feet.

"Sure." While his wife—boy was that going to take some getting used to—got ready for bed, he might as well get to work too. Tossing two pillows on the floor, he stepped out into the hall and grabbed a couple of blankets from the linen closet. Laying one down on the floor, he debated if he should have grabbed a comforter for more padding.

The bedroll set on the floor, the bathroom door inched open and wearing a bathrobe over her sweatpants and t-shirt, Sarah came to a stop. "What's this?"

"My bed."

Dropping her fists onto her hips, she frowned at him. "You're kidding?"

Without a word, he shook his head.

"You can't seriously tell me that you expect to sleep on

the floor for the next three hundred and sixty-four nights?"

"I do." His gaze drifted from the floor to the bed. "It's only a queen."

Her gaze narrowed further. "Are you telling me that I'm fat?"

"No!" His hands flew up in a defensive move. "Not at all." He gave a small smile. "You're perfect."

Her cheeks pinkened and her eyes softened. "Thank you, but you are not sleeping on the floor. That's as crazy as sleeping in the bathtub."

"Mom doesn't have a bathtub."

"You know what I mean." She crossed the room and pulled down the sheets on the side of the bed that still had pillows.

"You can sleep on the other side if you prefer." Preston stood still.

Shaking her head, Sarah walked around him and bent over to grab the pillows. "I promise to stick to my side." Still shaking her head, she shoved the two pillows into his gut. "No arguments."

He couldn't help himself, even though he'd never been in the military, he saluted her. "Yes, ma'am."

"And none of that ma'am stuff." Not looking his way, she slid under the covers, rolled over, her back to his side, and turned off the light. "Good night."

"Good night," he muttered back, briefly wondering what would be worse, sleeping close to Sarah Sue Conroy—now Sweet—or facing her wrath in the morning if he went ahead and slept on the floor?

CHAPTER THIRTEEN

"Hot coffee?" A carafe of fresh coffee in her hand, Sarah Sue stood by the kitchen table.

"Thanks." Carson held out his cup. "Don't tell Mom I said so, but your coffee is amazing."

"I heard that," the family matriarch's voice could be heard from the laundry room.

Rachel and Jillian chuckled at their mother's declaration. Sarah Sue, on the other hand, looked totally mortified.

On his feet, Preston took his plate to the stove and scooped two more spoonfuls of his mom's potato salad to go with the second helping of ribs already on his plate, then he leaned into where Sarah Sue stood. "You're doing great." Without thinking, he kissed her temple, delighted deep down when she smiled at him.

For over almost a month, still unable to secure lodging away from the ranch, they'd been playing the role of happy newlyweds for everyone. The thing that got Preston was that everything came so naturally. How they behaved in front of friends and family wasn't all that different from how they behaved when alone. He'd even gotten used to rolling over in his sleep and bumping into Sarah. A time or two…or three… he'd woken up with Sarah Sue curled into his side, or his arm around her. The only challenge had been resisting the urge to kiss her awake. That had not been part of the arrangement.

"Somebody spike your coffee?" Garret came to stand beside him at the stove.

"What?"

"You look like you sucked on a lemon or someone put

sour milk in your coffee."

Shaking his head, he wasn't quite sure what to say.

His brother, who'd returned from his summer camping trip a week ago, had been keeping an unusually close eye on Preston and Sarah Sue—at least that's how it felt to Preston. Garret rolled his eyes at his big brother. "Spit it out."

Now his brother sounded lost in some oral metaphor or food fixation.

"You're making faces. I know you're thinking about something other than the cows that keep escaping the south pasture."

Even though he wasn't thinking about that, the south pasture had been a thorn in their side for almost a month now. Every time they replaced a downed section, the cows would knock over another area. If they'd not actually continued to find all the wayward cattle, Preston would have sworn that Ray was behind the continued setbacks, but the south pasture had nothing to do with the thoughts currently running through his mind. "It's nothing."

"Trouble in paradise?" Garret teased.

The innocent jab shouldn't have struck a raw nerve, but it did. Preston bit down on his back teeth and willed the sharp words rushing to his tongue to settle down. "Paradise is just fine."

Garret shook his head and glanced over his brother's shoulder.

Unable to resist, Preston turned to see what had captured his brother's attention. The women seated at the kitchen table laughing and chatting over who knew what, brought a slight smile to his face. The family scene seemed so normal, so happy, and so…right.

"Mom," Garret called out. "I'm going to finish lunch on the back porch."

"No feeding Brady. He's starting to get a little thick around the middle."

"No, Ma'am." His brother shrugged an apology to the dog seated at his feet. "You heard her," he whispered to the devoted German Shepherd.

Preston would have sworn the dog sighed. Lately, he

was beginning to believe Brady was a human inside that fur coat.

"Join me, brother." Garret cocked his head toward the back door and didn't wait for a reply.

For as long as he could remember, whenever the siblings needed to work through something, whether personal or business, the best thinking and brainstorming was done at the table on the back porch. Even though they'd discussed the current family situation, including his and Sarah's marriage for the trust, ad nauseam, Preston knew it was time for one more conversation.

"Want to tell me now what you were thinking?" Garret settled into a seat and stabbed at his food.

"Not much."

"I call bullshit."

Preston didn't need a mirror to know his brows had just shot up kissing his hairline.

"Sorry. I may be younger than you are, but I can read that face like an open book."

"Grown up or not, Mom would wash your mouth out with soap if she heard you."

Garrett shrugged. "So what's eating you? For real?"

Did he dare tell his brother that this charade had become so real for him? That every time Sarah walked into a room his heart rate picked up? How every morning when he woke up before her, he felt like he'd died and gone to heaven?

"Is there a problem between you and Sarah?" Garret stabbed at his food before looking up. "From the first minute I heard of this crazy hare-brained idea I could see trouble coming, but honestly, y'all make it look easy."

"Thanks." Rather than say anything more, he slurped a long sip of his still hot coffee.

Garrett swallowed his food. "And a good thing too. That first trust payment was enough to buy some time with the bank and sprinkle a little seed money to keep an income coming in."

"That's the plan."

"But falling in love wasn't?"

If Preston's head had snapped up any faster, it would have rolled off his shoulders.

"It's pretty obvious this is not a school play."

He moved his mouth but nothing came out.

A small smile ticked at the corner of Garret's mouth. "Thought so." He sighed. "I debated if it was concern for who goes next and that there hasn't been a plan as plausible as yours and Sarah's, but this morning, when you kissed your wife and she smiled up at you, I saw it."

"It?"

"The same look Dad had every time Mom came near him. It was subtle, but there. And you have it."

On a sigh, he raked the fingers on both hands through his hair. "What am I going to do?"

Garrett shook his head. "This is just one reason why the whole pretend marriage idea is insane."

"But it's saved the ranch so far."

"And if one of us doesn't find a spouse willing to go along with this charade and get more money rolling in, it will all have been for nothing. We'll lose the ranch anyhow." Now Garret was the one who looked like he'd sucked on a lemon.

"Let me guess." Carson slid into the empty seat at the old patio table. "Planning who's next."

"I'm trying." Rachel kicked the kitchen door shut behind her. "It's not that easy finding people willing to put their lives on hold for a year."

"No kidding, Sherlock." Garret rolled his eyes.

"Men are such dogs."

"Excuse me?" Carson's eyes bulged from their sockets.

"Not you. Men I'm not related to."

"I don't get it." Garret shook his head. "What the heck are you talking about?"

Hands on her hips, she practically spit. "Sex."

Sarah Sue stepped out onto the porch with the others just as

Rachel practically ground out the word sex. Frozen in the doorway, she considered retreating into the house when her sort of sister-in-law waved at her.

"Come on out. There are no secrets in this family." Rachel took a sip of coffee and kicking her head back, sighed before looking over at her siblings. "I was just explaining to my brothers why men are dogs. Apparently, there are a lot of men willing to hook up for a price—and sex—but none so far are willing to keep things platonic for an entire year."

"Where are you finding these guys?" Garret nearly growled under a frown.

"Online. I created a fake profile and have been discreetly fishing. So to speak."

This wasn't the first time she'd heard her sister-in-law grumbling about finding a man to marry for money, but Rachel had never brought it up with her brothers.

"What about you two?" Rachel took another sip from her mug.

The way the two brothers stared down at their food in silence said everything.

"So you're not having any better luck either?"

Carson shook his head. "Let's just say the internet isn't as productive as I'd hoped."

"Ditto," Garret muttered.

Heaving a heavy sigh, Rachel turned to Sarah. "So, moving on, how's the dog placement business going?"

"Could be better."

"Fewer dogs?"

"That would help." Sarah chuckled. "It's just hard to find a home for the most difficult rescues."

"I bet. Brady wasn't easy when he first arrived. Recovering from his physical injuries was the simpler part." Carson's gaze shifted to the dog in question perched at the top of the porch steps, vigilantly surveying the horizon, prepared to do battle with any rodent or vermin who dared to encroach on his family's territory. "Somehow, Mom knew exactly how to deal with Brady's emotional challenges."

And that was why Sarah Sue had desperately wanted Alice Sweet to take on Samson. If Alice hadn't suffered painful injuries in her battle with a barbed wire fence, Sarah had no doubt that her mother-in-law would have been a perfect fit. But a hundred-pound dog with post-traumatic stress was not the kind of rest and recovery the doctor had in mind for Alice Sweet. At least the rescue ranch had found a suitable home for the troubled pup. She hoped he was as happy there as Brady seemed here.

"As a kid," Carson spoke up, "I thought Mom could do anything. As an adult, I haven't changed my mind."

All of Alice Sweet's children nodded. Sarah Sue felt the same way. It was going to take a miracle to bring the family ranch back to life, and with or without money, Alice Sweet was the only person Sarah Sue would place bets on.

For the next few minutes, the two single brothers chatted back and forth naming just about every single woman within a hundred-mile radius and so far, the conversation wasn't anymore productive than the previous conversations over the last month.

"You okay?" The soft brush of Preston's hand against hers, combined with the smooth timbre of his voice, had Sarah forgetting none of this was real, even if it felt very real to her.

Without a word, she bobbed her head.

His head tipped to one side, Preston's hand squeezed hers and he inched closer, his voice lower, intended only for her. "The look in your eyes tells me something's up."

There was no way she was going to share that what she'd feared had come to be. She'd fallen head over heels in love with Preston Sweet. "I was just thinking about Samson."

A frown settled between Preston's brows. "I thought they found a placement for him?"

"They did, but the more difficult ones always seem to needle their way into your heart a little more than the others. I was just hoping he's happy where he is now."

Lifting her hand to his smiling lips, Preston placed a barely there kiss. "That's just one of the things I love about you."

Love? *Love.* Stunned at the word, it took everything in her not to jump to conclusions. People love pizza, and sailing, and puppies, and movie marathons. The four-letter word was often tossed around and with little reverence to the big L.

As if a fly on the wall, ready to swoop in and save her from finding something intelligent to say, her phone rang and Aaron's name flashed across the screen.

"Speak of the devil." She plastered on a forced smile. "Probably calling with an update. Hey, Aaron. How's it going?"

"Samson is back."

"What?"

"Long story. The foster was an experienced German Shepherd owner, but totally unprepared for a dog with PTSD. If you thought he was stressed before, you wouldn't recognize him now."

"Poor baby." That just broke her heart.

"It gets worse. Yesterday, a volunteer dropped a bowl near Samson. The clatter of the metal dish spooked him and he lunged at her. Thankfully, she was close enough to the gate to escape unharmed, but…"

Pinching the bridge of her nose, she muttered "oh hell" and closed her eyes. She shouldn't have let the wedding rush distract her from placing Samson herself. Strong fingers curled around her shoulders. So caught up in the phone call, she hadn't noticed Preston push away from the table and come stand behind her. This man was simply too good to be true. If only he were really hers. "Aaron, buy me some time. We can fix this."

"I've bought this boy as much time as I can. All we've got is twenty-four more hours."

A few more words were exchanged and she disconnected the call, knowing she had to move fast to save Samson—and she was going to need Alice's help to do it.

CHAPTER FOURTEEN

"Though difficult, Samson wasn't deemed dangerous," Sarah Sue explained. "But now, he's crossed the line."

Alice Sweet frowned at her new daughter-in-law. Oh, how she liked those words. Daughter-in-law. Though everything happened unusually fast, and Alice had had her share of doubts along the way, deep down she was a romantic at heart who believed in love at first sight— maybe—but for now they had a new problem on their hands. "But he didn't bite the woman."

"He might as well have." Heaving a deep sigh, Sarah inched forward. "Samson doesn't do well with other dogs. As you know, none of the former service dogs that fail out of Lackland AFB can be placed in a home with young children, so that eliminates a good many foster wannabes, and after this fail with an experienced GSD owner, the Sweet Ranch is his only hope."

"Agreed." Leaning back in her seat, Alice had a determined look on her face. "I'll round up the boys and we'll get a place ready for Samson that will keep him apart from Brady, at least for now. But you'd better hurry, the forecast for tonight isn't good."

"Don't I know it." Sarah sighed. "First thing I did after speaking to Aaron was check the forecast. We need to rescue Samson before the heavier storms reach the rescue ranch. If he's regressed, even the smallest of thunderstorms could be a nightmare for the poor dog."

"Like I said," Alice pushed to her feet, "you'd better hurry. I think we have an old kennel in the garage if you need it. You also might want to grab a blanket off your bed.

Maybe a shirt too. Things with your scent that might help keep the pup calm on the long drive."

"Good idea." Sarah Sue bobbed her head quickly. Alice didn't have to be a mind reader to know that her new daughter-in-law was mentally running through what she might need.

"I'll get the keys to the Suburban." Preston took a step back. "If we're going to bring Samson home in a kennel, we'll need a vehicle big enough to transport him that way."

"Perfect." Sarah Sue let go of the door handle. "I'll run up and grab a blanket. Riding home surrounded by our scent will help with the transition."

Grabbing the keys off the hook by the kitchen door, he leaned over and kissed Sarah Sue on the temple before hurrying out of the house.

The tender gesture made Alice smile. How she was loving watching those two together. "Go save that baby." She shot Sarah Sue a thumbs up moments before the door closed behind her son and Sarah Sue bolted up the stairs.

Waiting for Sarah Sue to hurry downstairs again, Alice gathered Brady's spare collar and leash. Just in case. The poor dog might not be thrilled with the scent of another animal, but a blind introduction couldn't hurt. As soon as her son's bride scurried through the kitchen, Alice gave her the collar and leash. "Just in case Samson doesn't already have one. And here." She shoved two bottles of water at them and a small bag of treats. "As you know, water and treats can work wonders to making fast friends with a stressed K-9."

Arms full, Sarah paused and leaned over to give her mother-in-law a peck on the cheek. "You're the best."

"Ditto." Ever since Sarah Sue lost her mom, Alice had felt a responsibility to her friend, neighbor, and their daughter. Having Sarah Sue hanging around the house often with Jillian and Rachel had been like having a third daughter. Stepping in to help Doc when he had no idea what to do with a heartbroken teen or burgeoning young woman, had come as naturally as dealing with her own daughters. She'd hoped that one of her sons would fall for the incredible woman Sarah Sue had become. Troubled dog and thunderstorms aside, Alice couldn't be any happier for Preston. "Well, Charlie. One down and five to go. I just hope they all find someone as perfect for them as Sarah Sue is for Preston."

Every few minutes, the tendrils of lightening stretched across the sky, illuminating the road ahead for miles. For Samson and Sarah Sue's sake, Preston prayed the storm didn't reach the rescue ranch, or dealing with a traumatized dog was going to be twice as hard as he already anticipated.

Another hour into the drive, and rather than the heavens clearing up, the sky sounded as angry as it looked.

"Poor baby is probably totally freaking out with this storm." Sarah stared upward as if willing the storm to pass them by sooner than later.

"I'm sure Aaron is doing all he can to keep the dog from stressing."

"Sometimes," her gaze remained on the light show ahead, "no matter how badly we want it, no matter how hard a person wishes it away, the invisible scars of war can't be controlled. Every flash of lightening and roar of thunder grabs hold of good service men and dogs deep in their gut and drags them back to a living nightmare."

Preston's mind flashed over to his brother. Every leave, every trip home, there seemed to be a small part of Kade that changed a little here, then there. Usually, after spending time with the family, Kade almost seemed his old self, but there was always a bit of harshness that still broke through, reminding everyone of the career their brother would be returning to. Preston couldn't help but wonder how much longer before they lost all trace of the tender-hearted side of the older brother who'd seen too much of the ugliness in the world.

"Worrying about Samson?" Her gaze had shifted to him, and a concerned softness seemed to have settled on him.

"A little, but mostly I was thinking about Kade."

"What about him?"

"Life. War. And someday coming home for good."

Her head leaned back. "Someday soon, I hope."

"Ditto."

For the rest of the drive, barely a word or two had been exchanged. Thoughts of Kade and Samson swirled silently in their heads. Sight of the rescue ranch lit up under a crash of thunder that sounded to be hovering directly over them. When Preston pulled up to the spot Aaron had told them to come to, Sarah Sue bolted from the vehicle before he'd had time to shove the gear shift into park. At least the Texas light show hadn't brought any rain so far. A downpour would only make bringing Samson home more difficult.

Several yards ahead of him, Sarah Sue and Aaron were already toe to toe in conversation; Aaron, bobbing his head and pointing, while Sarah Sue most likely was giving orders.

"So we're in agreement?" Sarah Sue stood arms crossed in front of her friend.

"I may agree, but that doesn't mean I have to like it."

Without knowing the details, Preston already knew, whatever it was Aaron didn't like, Preston probably wouldn't like it either. Before he'd come fully to her side, Sarah Sue turned on her heels and trotted toward where Aaron had been pointing. "What don't you like?" he asked.

"She wants to approach Samson alone."

"What?" His voice came out louder than he'd intended.

"Anyone else and I'd have said absolutely not."

"You still should have." Going in to face a scared, stressed, and vicious dog on her own was not sitting well with Preston, not at all.

Aaron turned to face Preston, his brows slowly curling into a perfect V shape. "How long have you known this woman?"

"Long enough."

"At this point, nothing could make things any worse than they are. Feel free to go see for yourself."

"I will." Preston hadn't made it more than a foot or two

when Aaron called after him.

"Just don't get too close to her. If she sees you, Samson won't be the vicious one you need to worry about."

Her head down, her gaze cast toward the ground, Sarah was very slowly undoing the chain on a large lone kennel separating Samson from all the other dogs and activity on site.

All Preston could do was hold his breath; if he shouted at her now, he'd probably just agitate Samson even more. The second the gate slowly swung open, Samson crouched down on his front paws. Not a good thing. The animal was clearly preparing to pounce.

"Remember me, boy?" Sarah's voice came out slow and smooth. "We're going to be good friends."

What the heck was she thinking, entering into a cage with an out of control animal and not a lick of protection? Not a stick, not a tranquilizer, no protective padding, nada. Just her and the dog, and oh hell, now the whites of snarling teeth could be seen by a blind man. He couldn't help himself, as softly and calmly as he could muster, he spoke for Sarah Sue to hear. "Please step back, let me help."

Without hesitation, she barely shook her head. In the darkness, he couldn't swear in a court of law, but he was pretty darn sure she'd just shot him a deadly glare. Aaron was right, she could be as dangerous as the dog.

The fur along Samson's spine stood upright, and to prove his mood to all bystanders, Samson added a fearsome growl to the exposed fangs. Regardless of what she wanted, the hackles on the back of Preston's neck were rising too. Ripping off his shirt, he wrapped it around his one arm and slowly eased closer, praying that Samson wouldn't attack before he reached his wife. Any other time and he would pause to let that word roll around his tongue—he'd begun to get used to it, but now was most definitely not the time to lose focus.

The gate open just wide enough for Sarah to slink into the enclosure, Preston still several yards away, Samson seemed to shift from paw to paw and they both knew what was coming next. One hundred pounds of angry fur-covered muscle lunged toward Sarah Sue and the gate.

Setting all caution aside, Preston bolted toward the kennel, reaching the entry just as Sarah Sue stumbled backward, failing to latch the gate before Samson shoved it forward, knocking her into Preston's arms.

"Crap." Sarah Sue sprang to her feet and without a word, took off at a full gallop after the dog.

"Wait." Preston chased after her. He might have nearly a foot on the woman, but she ran with the speed of an Olympic track star. "Sarah Sue!"

"We have to find him before he hurts himself."

It wasn't the dog getting hurt he was worried about.

Before Preston could move a step, Aaron came running behind him. "Here. Take the jeep. Adrenaline can have him running fast and far."

"Thanks." Preston snatched the proffered keys to the vehicle parked a few feet away and hurried to catch up with Sarah. "Climb in."

Scrambling to a halt, she grabbed on and swung into the seat. "Go."

The dog had disappeared from sight. Preston slowed, scanning the surroundings.

"There!" Sarah pointed to the dark shadow ahead from a mound of dead wisteria. The white fangs and whites of frantic eyes could be seen peering out at them from between the barren twigs.

Once again the Jeep hadn't come to a complete stop when she bolted. He was going to have to talk to her about that.

Grabbing a large blanket from the back seat, Preston trotted around the front of the hood and grabbed her arm, gently yanking her to a halt. "Let me. I've worked with Brady, and if he lunges, at least I have some protection."

A jagged ray of light stretched from sky to ground at the same moment the clap of thunder sounded overhead followed by the cracking sound of breaking wood. Lightning had struck a nearby tree. A dead tree. The crackling sound continued until a loud thud of a branch slamming against the ground filled the air. And something else.

Even Samson sensed it. All three had raised their noses to the air. The smell was unmistakable. Smoke. And fire.

Flames shot up high from the struck tree, sparks began flying in every direction. Like a match on gas-soaked kindling, fires erupted left and right, rivers of flames traveling from dry spot to spot.

"Damn it." Preston surveyed their surroundings. The fire was spreading fast, too fast. If they didn't move, and soon, they'd be trapped. "We have to go. Give me the leash, I'll get the dog. You take the Jeep and I'll catch up."

"No. We'll do this together."

"Sarah Sue."

"Look." She pointed ahead. "He's coming out."

"Smart dog. Now go. I'll handle this."

"Together. We'll handle this."

"Sarah Sue. Please."

Ignoring him, she inched closer to the dog, only this time, instead of raging with fear and anger, the dog was slinking slowly forward, his gaze darting from them to the flames expanding around them. This was so not good.

CHAPTER FIFTEEN

She should have listened. Even though her instincts had told her that Samson would calm down with her, Preston was right, she should have let him have her back. Maybe then they wouldn't be standing in the middle of a fast-growing brush fire with a traumatized dog.

"Smoke's getting thick." Preston stared into the distance. "I'm going to circle around and toss the blanket on Samson. Then I'll scoop him up and we'll both head for the Jeep. Agreed?"

As much as she hated it, she shook her head and pointed to the vehicle now parked on the other side of the blazing fire.

Eyes blinked shut, Preston blew out a sigh. The blanket balled under one arm, his other fist clenched at his side.

Samson whimpered, easing closer.

"He seems calmer." Though she had absolutely no idea why an animal that moments ago was frenzied with stress now seemed to be focused and absurdly calm.

Black smoke was growing thick and strong.

"This smoke can overtake us in a heartbeat. We need to get down." Tugging her to the ground, the way Preston's gaze darted about, she knew he was doing the same thing she was—debating how the heck they were going to get out of here.

Another bolt of lightening flashed in the sky accompanied by the crash of thunder, but unlike before, Samson remained settled, calm, his nose twitching from the scents around him. Suddenly, the animal tipped his head back, howled, and ran circles around the two of them. Could it be possible the fire had driven the dog completely over the edge and off his rocker?

"What do you have in your pockets?" Crouching on his knees, he pulled out one of the bottles of water his mother had given them.

"Treats, water, and a pocket knife."

"Pocket knife?"

She shrugged. "You never know when it might come in handy."

"Right now I'd kill for a shovel."

"Shovel?"

He tipped his chin behind them. "Winds moving the fire towards us."

"Yeah." She'd noticed too. All the firefighting training in the world wouldn't do Preston any good without the right tools. Trying her best not to panic, she couldn't help but think if ever panic was in order, this situation would be it.

Somehow, Preston had to get Sarah out of this. Digging a hole by hand wasn't going to work. If they had a shovel, there was a small chance that if they sank into the ground and covered themselves with a water-soaked blanket, the fire might blow over them. And right about now, a small chance was better than no chance. But the problem remained: no shovel.

Samson howled again, did another circle dance and this time darted forward before coming back and howling again.

"He's getting worked up again," Sarah almost whispered.

No one could blame the animal.

"Preston." Sarah nibbled on her lower lip.

"Got a good idea?"

Shaking her head, she leaned in. "I just want to say something, in case, you know, if we don't get out."

"Don't say that. Don't even think it." He was thinking it enough for the both of them.

She blew out a deep sigh. "I love you."

If it were possible for time to stop, it just had, along with his heart.

"I know that wasn't the plan, but I don't want to die without you knowing."

Gently, he took her hand in his and pulled her closer. "First, we're not going to die," even if he had to carry them through the fire to fulfill that promise, "and second, I love you more."

A slight grin tugged at the corners of her mouth. "I love you most."

Before he could come up with an appropriate comeback, Samson lunged at them, grabbing hold of Preston's pants leg and tugging him away. "Don't tell me he's jealous." That's all he needed, for the frantic dog to get over his PTSD and then come between him and Sarah.

This had to be something more. Samson's frantic energy was palpable, his brown eyes wide and locked on Preston's, as if willing him to understand. The dog released his grip and barked sharply, then darted a few feet away, pausing to look back, his tail wagging in rapid, desperate sweeps.

Sarah grabbed hold of Preston's arm. "He wants us to follow him."

Could it be? "I think you're right."

Samson barked again, circling in agitation before sprinting to a thicket of trees. He barked twice more and jumped up, his paws scrabbling at the bark of one particularly sturdy-looking oak.

Smoke billowed in a choking cloud. Crouching low to the ground, he moved forward, following the dog, pulling Sarah with him.

"Preston…" with the heat licking at their backs, Sarah's voice trembled, her grip tightening on his arm. "Do you think he—"

"I don't know, but we're out of options."

Scrambling toward the determined dog, they were almost close enough to touch him when Samson suddenly bolted past the tree and into a narrow, barely discernible opening between the thick underbrush. Preston squinted, trying to make out where the dog was leading them. Obscured by dense foliage, the opening had yet to be engulfed by the fire.

"If this dog has found a way out, he's getting the biggest bone the butcher has for dinner." Preston tugged on Sarah's hand, hurrying them along.

"And breakfast too," her voice stronger, sounded more hopeful.

Disappearing into the brush, Samson's barks echoed back to them. Still crouching low to avoid overhanging branches, they scurried after him. Air was heavy with smoke, mingled with oppressive heat, making it hard to breathe. Ahead the narrow passage seemed to curve away from the flames.

"I knew he was a special dog. He's leading us away from the fire," Sarah gasped, glancing over her shoulder. "How does he know?"

Preston shook his head. "Honestly, I haven't a clue how he knows, I'm just glad he does. We've got to keep moving."

Following the distant sound of Samson's barks, they pressed on. The smell of smoke stronger than before, Preston said a silent prayer that they weren't following the dog to their deaths.

Holding her shirt up over her nose and mouth, Sarah stumbled on a root, her hands flailing, Preston caught her, the force of her weight propelling them to the ground. Overhead he could see sparks spinning through space, tossed about by the gusts of wind. They needed to push ahead, faster, before the sparks rained down around them and set this corner of their world into another fiery blaze.

Scratched and scraped from crawling through the dry thicket, Samson's howl drew them forward until they burst into a small clearing. The ground marshy and thick with mud, Samson stood barking at the edge of a narrow creek.

The fire still raging behind them, Preston almost laughed at the sight of Samson prancing in the cool water. "Smart dog."

Samson barked again, whether in agreement or still directing them, Preston didn't know or care. They'd followed the dog this far, no sense in stopping now. Splashing through the shallow water, the coolness covered them in blessed relief against the scorching heat.

"Good boy, Samson," Sarah encouraged the dog.

Above, the whirling sound of aircraft engines roared, followed by waves of water showering the distant flames.

"Thank God," Sarah whispered.

The trio followed the creek past the burning brush and around the curving bends until they could see the rescue ranch in the distance. Out of the water, Samson trotted ahead, his tail wagging triumphantly.

Adrenaline waning, exhaustion reared its head, dropping Preston to his knees. Beside him, Sarah sank to the ground.

Samson stood for a long moment staring back at them as if asking, *you're stopping now?* before turning and galloping back to where they sat, exhausted. When the happy dog came up beside Sarah and licked her face enthusiastically, she threw her arms around him. "Foster my foot. You're ours."

"Amen." Preston stretched his hand to scratch behind the dog's ears. He didn't want to think what would have happened if the dog had not managed to clamp down his anxiety and slip into working dog mode. Though Preston doubted escaping blazing fires had ever been in the job description, at this moment, he'd believe anything, including super dog and guardian angel.

Alice Sweet hovered over her son like a new mother watching her infant sleeping. Sarah's father wasn't much better. Together in the Sweet family living room, sitting side by side on the sofa, Preston and Sarah had little say in the matter as both parents insisted they stay wrapped in quilts, drink lots of hot chocolate, and if they brought out one more thing for them to eat, Sarah was going back to face the fire again—an easier adversary than their two parents.

When they finally found themselves blessedly alone, as if choreographed, they both threw off the blankets and Sarah leaned into Preston's side as his arm draped around her, tugging her more closely against him.

Warm lips pressed against her temple. "I love you, Mrs. Sweet."

The words were music to her soul. Lifting her gaze to meet his, she took in the love shining in his eyes. He meant it. "I was afraid it was the adrenaline talking."

His head shook from side to side as his lips came down on hers. The gentle warmth spread from her mouth to her toes as he pulled her impossibly closer. They'd shared plenty of kisses for show, but this was most definitely so very different. Her toes were almost curling in her shoes.

"Oops." His mom stopped short, her shoes clacking a fast exit back to the kitchen.

Chuckling, they pulled apart.

"We really do need to find our own place." Preston ran his thumb down her cheek.

Sucking in a long, deep breath, Sarah blew it out slowly. "As Mr. and Mrs.?"

"If you meant what you said?"

Her head bobbed. "I did."

"For better or worse, till death do us part." No sooner had the words left his lips then his face pinched. "Sorry, poor choice of words."

"Perfect words. From this day forward, you're stuck with me."

"Sounds like heaven." He leaned in for another kiss when a nearby deep voice cleared his throat.

"Maybe you two should take this upstairs?" Carson bit back a smile and winked.

Preston locked gazes with her and any other day she would have raced him up the stairs, but tonight, there was someplace else she wanted to be. As if reading her mind, Preston nodded.

They had one meaty bone to deliver to their favored guest set up in the barn's best accommodation.

In perfect unison, their two voices chorused, "Samson."

EPILOGUE

"Good grief." Alice Sweet blinked. "I think I've been permanently blinded."

Carson couldn't help but snicker. His mom's exaggeration wouldn't be so amusing if it weren't pretty much true. On a good day, Mildred McEntire could out sparkle the North Star, but today's bedazzled outfit could definitely light the way for a parade of tankers on a foggy night. The woman had outdone herself. Form-fitting stretch pants with a matching sweat jacket in neon pink could grab anyone's attention, but the fine lines of silver beads and sequins that ran side by side from top to bottom set the suit apart from anything Carson had ever seen in his life, including on prom night. There were probably several drag queens who would kill for that outfit. All she needed was a pair of platform sparkled shoes and she could own the runway. The thought of Mildred surrounded by a multitude of strutting drag queens had him biting down on his lower lip.

"It's not funny." His mother rubbed her eyes.

"No, ma'am."

"Every time she swings that arm, the reflection of the sun hits everyone. Give her a magnifying glass and she could start a fire."

This time, a loud laugh burst from deep inside him.

Alice Sweet flashed her son a practiced glare that he hadn't seen since he was a teenager.

"Sorry."

"Hm," his mom grunted. "I think she's doing it on purpose. Then no one will be able to see well enough to get the bean bags in the holes."

Normally, he would have argued that the declaration was a bit much, but in this case, he wouldn't put it past Mildred.

"Did we miss much?" Sarah Sue came hurrying up beside them, Preston on her heels. "We were waiting to bring Dad, but he got called away to the Hanson place; one of the twins sliced his chin open falling from a tree."

"Oh, dear." His mom spun around.

Sarah Sue smiled. "If the way he was cussing out his brother for pushing him is any indication, I'd venture it could have been worse. Dad said it would be faster for him to drive to the ranch to stitch the kid up than meeting them at his office. Especially with everyone and their godmother in town for the tournament."

"Well, I'm glad the fall wasn't any worse." Alice turned back just as her sister Vicki weighed the bean bags in her hand. "Ooh. It's our turn."

Standing only inches behind his wife, Preston gently laid his hands on her shoulders and kissed the top of her head. When she leaned back into him, his arms dropped and circled her waist. They looked like two perfectly fitting puzzle pieces. A rush of delight at his brother's newfound happiness warmed Carson's heart at the same time a sense of dread squeezed his chest.

Preston had found the brass ring. A temporary wife for the good of the family had become the perfect match, the love of his life. There was no way Carson would be that lucky, or as his mother would often say, blessed. At this rate, one of them had to find someone—anyone—to marry and fast. The money Preston had been gifted by the trust was already spent and the small monthly stipend was helping, but they needed more. A lot more. And the lawsuit over the development still had all his money tied up for who knew how much longer. Like it or not, he was going to have to bite the bullet and pick a woman, any woman.

"She made it." His mom slapped her hands together with glee then cupping her mouth, hollered at her other sister, Liz, who was up next.

Sarah Sue put her fingers to her lips and let out a

whistle that could probably have been heard all the way in Oklahoma. While Carson resisted the urge to rub his ears, Preston leaned in and kissed his bride as if there was no one else on the planet.

A sharp elbow jabbed him in the side. Spinning his head around, he leveled his gaze with his sister Jillian.

"It's not nice to stare. Give them some privacy."

"Privacy?" Did she not know there were at least a thousand people mulling about for the weekend tournament? It was all he could manage not to shout at the newlyweds to get a room.

"They really are cute." Jillian cast a sideways glance in their direction and the hint of a smile, bloomed into a full grin. "They remind me of Mom and Dad."

Daring to turn to face his sibling and his wife, Carson's gaze dropped to their now joined hands. It was as if they always had to be touching. Either fingertips, or shoulders, or knees. His sister was right, the two were so dang much in love, any fool could see it. And yes, he had no doubt these two would develop the same kind of bond their parents had. The corker: not till this very moment did he realize just how much he wanted the same thing. For just a split moment, his mind darted back to college and the one woman whose memory had stuck with him all these years. Too bad she was married to another man.

"Any luck?" Jillian muttered softly.

There was no need to ask with what. He merely shook his head. Luck and love had eluded him all this time, why should it find him now?

"She did it!" Their mother spun about on her heels again, threw her arms up in the air before pulling all her kids into a huddled hug. "They made it to the semi-finals!"

Easing out of the family squeeze, Carson's gaze homed in on Preston and Sarah Sue, walking hand in hand, gently bumping hips with every other step, as they joined his mom in congratulating her sisters. A slow sigh escaped from deep in his lungs.

"Yeah." Jillian sighed beside him. "I know how you feel."

Everyone, including his aunts, were doing what they could to save the Sweet Ranch. It was time he stopped dragging his feet. Somewhere in the plethora of women who had responded to his postings there had to be one that would be able to pull off the charade for a year without making his life miserable. There just had to be.

Enjoy an excerpt from
Sweet Surprise

"So, are we getting a new sister-in-law?" En route across their father's office, Rachel paused to kiss Carson Sweet on the cheek, then collapsing into her favorite chair, finger by finger, tugged off her driving gloves.

"Not exactly." Desperation and relief tumbled about in Carson's gut.

Frozen, tugging on her last finger, Rachel stared at him. "What do you mean, not exactly?"

Garret leaned forward. "I thought you said you were going to propose last night."

"I was."

"She said no?" Jillian's eyes rounded before she blew out a deep sigh.

"I never asked."

"Oh." Rachel whipped off the glove and leaned back. "So you're going to ask tonight."

Carson shook his head. "It's probably for the best, but last night before our date, she FaceTimed to announce that her troublesome ex had appeared on her doorstep with not one but two dozen roses and a diamond ring the size of Gibraltar—how could she say no?"

"Well, crap." Rachel tossed her gloves aside.

"Sorry we're late." Like young teens with hands clasped practically skipping into the room, Preston took a seat on the leather sofa, his wife Sarah Sue sitting beside him. Of course, still holding hands.

"How are you liking the new living arrangements?" Jillian looked up from pouring herself a cola.

"Not bad at all." Preston smiled.

"Not bad?" His wife frowned at him. "It's perfectly lovely. When Clint and your mom said they were going to makeover one of the unused bunkhouses, I had visions of living like a college dorm."

Rachel smiled. "I'm guessing Mom had other ideas?"

"Yep." Sarah Sue bobbed her head. "The kitchen and table were already there, but opening up the living area by combining it with one of the bunk rooms makes the space seem so roomy."

"It's always boggled my mind how Mom can envision beauty from junk." Jillian took a sip of her drink and turned to Carson. "I'm guessing that's where you inherited it from?"

Lost in his own thoughts, it took Carson a moment to realize his sister was talking to him. "Sorry?"

Jillian rolled her eyes. "You're a good real estate investor because you learned how from Mom."

"Oh. yeah. Mom always has great ideas." Too bad she wasn't in on their plans to offer him up an idea of how to find and marry a wife quickly so he could collect on the stupid trust and help save the ranch.

"So," Rachel crossed her legs, "what do we do now?"

"Have either of you men considered an old girlfriend? Surely there's a still single one floating around somewhere?"

Two heads moved from side to side.

Garret heaved a sigh. "What about you girls? You two were very popular in high school. No prospects on that end? Even a friend would do."

It seemed to Carson that they were all just spinning their wheels. This same conversation had been had over and over for the last few weeks. Nothing new had come from any of it.

"Maybe we should just tell Mom the truth and see if she gets on board with the plan." Garret waved toward Preston and Sarah Sue. "After all, it worked out for you two. Maybe that would make Mom more willing?"

"No!" multiple voices echoed in precise and adamant

chorus.

Jillian leaned back in her seat and waved her glass at the youngest brother in the family. "Just because true love struck the first time out does not mean Mom would go along with us trying again. Not to mention she's a rule follower and a pretend marriage to gain access to the trust could be considered fraud."

"Not could be," Carson interjected, "is."

"She's right." Rachel pushed to her feet and crossed to the mini fridge at the bar. "Mom cannot know."

Frustrated and tired, Carson stood as well. "I need to pick up an order from the feed store and then I'm meeting Chet Barker for lunch."

"Chet? You haven't seen him in years."

"I know. His dad had a heart attack so Chet's come to see him. I think he's suffering from a guilty conscience after moving so far away."

"Hey, didn't he have a rather pretty sister you were sweet on?" Rachel's brows curled into a deep V.

Carson shrugged. He wasn't exactly sweet on Carolyn Barker, but she was awfully easy on the eyes and her sense of humor could turn a bad day around. "I thought I'd catch up on how Carolyn's doing. Maybe that could be an option."

"Now you're talking." Jillian smiled. "Second chance at romance could work with Mom."

Again, Carson shrugged. All the siblings had come to understand that unlike Sarah Sue, who agreed to marry Preston for the family, any woman—or man—who consented to be wed for a year was going to need at least some financial compensation. Maybe if he was lucky, Carolyn was not only single, but looking for an easy way to earn a down payment on a condo somewhere.

This couldn't be happening. Jessica Pratt sat across from the doctor's desk, waiting impatiently for the bad news. Ever since her ex had shown up drunk as a skunk, pounding on her door at the stroke of midnight, her world had turned even more upside down than it had been since Todd walked out on his family, cleaning out their bank accounts on the way to the divorce lawyer. She'd not wanted to let him in, but when he broke down crying on the other side of her door, muttering he was sick, how could she leave him out there?

Four cups of coffee later, she'd learned just how sick. Todd Pratt had Huntington's disease. His dad had died at a young age from the illness, but he and his mother had hoped that showing no signs of it by the same age, Todd would not have inherited the dreadful gene. Apparently, hope wasn't worth much.

It had taken her hours after he left to finally give up on getting any sleep. While she wanted nothing to do with the good-for-little ex-husband, he had given her a precious boy, and would need someone to look after him. His mother was young and had been through this once, and his sister was available to help, but Jessica couldn't shake the guilt that despite his character flaws, she still felt sorry for him.

Of course, she didn't get far with that internal debate when she began to worry about her own son. What if Colton had inherited the same ugly disease? The thought of her little boy someday having his life cut horribly short had her crying into her pillow for hours.

For the next few weeks, she went through the motions of day to day living, in the back of her mind debating what to do next. Of course, when the time came and Todd needed more care, she should step up and help the father of her only child. But, after finding herself more and more unsettled with each passing day, rumors were flying that layoffs were coming. She already struggled to keep up with expenses and feed her son, everything seemed so danged uncertain, and now this revelation hung over her like a guillotine waiting to fall. Finally she decided she couldn't handle not knowing, was not the kind of person who could go through life just waiting for a genetic mutation to strike. Knowing if Colton carried the gene was better than waiting for the other shoe to fall.

Which brought her full circle to today. She'd found a specialist who agreed to do the testing on Colton. A simple process that she'd had to run up her credit card for, but it had to be done. The not knowing was eating away at her. The only challenge now was the phone call from the nurse. She could still hear the soft-spoken woman's voice replaying in her head.

"Mrs. Pratt? Dr. Sullivan would like to discuss your son's test results in person. When would you be available to come in?"

In person. What awful fate awaited Colton that Dr. Sullivan couldn't simply say yes or no? Then her mind ran around with every worse case scenario from Colton was already showing symptoms she hadn't noticed, to some other deadly disease was found in his genetic makeup. It hadn't helped her nerves any that it had taken four weeks to get the initial consultation with Dr. Sullivan and now he was willing to squeeze her in anytime rather than wait.

Not able to stand another minute with her terrified imagination, she'd taken the afternoon off of work—if it cost her her job, so be it—and hurried to the doctor's office. Two hours later she'd been moved from the lobby to his office, but was still waiting. In her lap, the confetti of tissue paper she'd methodically twisted and tugged, was the only visible sign of just how scared she was.

"Sorry for the delay, Mrs. Pratt."

"I appreciate you squeezing me in like this."

"Yes." An older man with salt and pepper hair and just enough padding to be considered jolly, slid into his seat and opened a folder. Perusing through several pages, he pulled out a sheet and setting it in front of him, steepled his fingers. "I recently diagnosed your husband—"

"Ex-husband," she interrupted.

"Yes. Ex-husband who has Huntington's."

She bobbed her head, willing herself to stop shredding what was left of the tissue in her hand.

"First of all, I am very happy to tell you that your son does not have any sign of inheriting the diseased gene."

A thousand pound anvil slid away from her shoulders. "That's wonderful news." Except the doctor wasn't smiling. "What else is wrong?"

The doctor picked up the paper in front of him. "Because I am your ex-husband's physician, he agreed to have the same DNA testing done as we performed on your son."

Again, her head nodded slowly.

"I don't mean to be indiscreet, but are you aware that Colton is not your ex's biological son?"

What? Not Todd's son? But…

"I'm guessing by that deer in the headlight expression, the answer is no?"

She slowly nodded. The only reason she'd married Todd was when she'd learned she was pregnant.

"I see. Well," the man cleared his throat, "if you need to have me run any further testing, perhaps the father, just let me know."

This time she could only blink. Perhaps the father. She'd only slept with one other man the entire time she and Todd were dating. One time. One Man. Holy Mary mother of Jesus, Carson Sweet was Colton's father.

Read more of Sweet Surprise available now

MEET CHRIS

USA TODAY Bestselling Author of dozens of contemporary novels, including the award winning Aloha Series, Chris Keniston lives in suburban Dallas with her husband, two human children, and two canine children. Though she loves her puppies equally, she admits being especially attached to her German Shepherd rescue. After all, even dogs deserve a happily ever after.

More on Chris and all her books can be found at
www.chriskeniston.com

Follow Chris' Monday Blog at her website
ChrisKenistonAuthor

Follow Chris on Facebook at
ChrisKenistonAuthor

Never miss a New Release!
Sign up for News from Chris:
www.chriskeniston.com/newsletter.html

Questions? Comments?
I would love to hear from you! You can reach me at:
chris@chriskeniston.com

9 798891 490284